# Fire Fang

Witch Haven Cozy Mystery - book 13

## K.E. O'Connor

K.E. O'Connor Books

# Preface

The Witch Haven series has been created so you spend time with four amazing witches:

**Books 1-3** tell Indigo's story: Spells and Spooks, Hexes and Haunts, Curses and Corpses

**Books 4-6** tell Luna's story: Muffins and Moonlight, Cupcakes and Cauldrons, Pancakes and Potions

**Books 7-9** tell Odessa's story: Hauntings and High Jinx, Hauntings and Havoc, Hauntings and Hoaxes

**Books 10-12** tell Storm's story: The Case of the Screaming Skull, The Case of the Poisoned Pumpkin, The Case of the Cursed Candy

And there are two bonus origin stories to enjoy:

**Fire Fang** and **Silvaria**

# Chapter 1

"How does this magic system work?"

I had my hands squashed under my thighs to resist the urge to clench my fists. This was my third therapist in six months, and each of them had reacted in the same way when I'd told them about my intense magical dreams and visions. Mild surprise, amusement, and then resignation. Here we go again, another loser with no life.

"Noah? I'm interested. You need to open up to get any benefit from these sessions." My therapist, Doctor Tom Saunders, please, call me Tom, was about my age, in his mid-thirties, neat hair, tidy suit, red tie, with the top button of his white shirt undone to show he was professional but not uptight.

"You really want to know?" I said.

"It would be useful to both of us. It's good to talk about these things. It's why I'm here."

I shrugged. "The magic isn't infinite. If spells are cast or potions used, they drain the magic user. Magic has a cost. It's basic magical lore." I cringed. Total nerd geek comment.

Tom had the decency not to smirk, but it looked like a struggle. "Of course. We don't want witches and wizards casting their spells with abandon. What would us mere mortals do? Roll the dice and see if our number let us raise a shield spell?"

"It's not Dungeons and Dragons. Not role play. It exists." What I saw wasn't in my head. But if it wasn't a hallucination, where was it coming from, and why could no one else see it? "It would make more sense if I didn't know any of this was real. Imagine the panic if everyone knew magic existed, yet we didn't have it, so we couldn't keep ourselves safe?"

"Which suggests what to you?"

I clenched my teeth. "That magic isn't real?"

"Right." Tom's pen was poised over his pad, hoping something meaningful would come out of my mouth that he could scribble down and dissect. "Tell me more about the magical codes."

I tried to relax. I needed this outlet, or I'd stop functioning. And this was all confidential, so he couldn't joke about me to his wife or friends. Hopefully. "You need rules for any way of living. It would have to be illegal for people who had magic to use it on those who didn't."

"Why do you think that?"

"It's the same as armed police going into a crowd of peaceful protestors. They have an unfair advantage. They could control us with magic. Do what they liked to us."

"Is that something you're interested in? You want someone to have power over you and tell you what to do?"

My fingers flexed under my thighs. Tom was looking for the reason I had these delusions. He was doing his job, but these therapists were all the same. Rather than supporting my imagination and open-mindedness, they squashed it and looked for some deep psychological issue.

I didn't know if I agreed with past trauma making me believe in magic, but something was wrong with me. Otherwise, I wouldn't be here for the fourth time this month.

But just once, it would be amazing to talk to someone who was willing to consider the possibility magic existed, and living in a world where magic was real would be better than the world I lived in.

Silence stretched out for a minute before Tom adjusted his tie and clicked his pen. "How are you getting on with cutting back on your working hours?" He flicked through his notes. "Are you still working seventy-hour weeks?"

"My work isn't the problem. I love my job."

"Designing games for online platforms? Do the games involve magic?"

"It's what I'm known for. My boss, Gideon Masters, poached me because my Enchanted Forests of Avalon game was so popular. It was optioned around the world, and there's a spin-off series being made for TV."

"Congratulations. I've never played it."

"You'd enjoy it. But you need to believe in magic to get the most out of it. It's based on the legend of King Arthur. And there are dragons."

"Like you? Do you really believe in magic? Don't the laws of science make it impossible?"

"The best scientists are the ones working to disprove their own theories."

This earned me a smile. "Perhaps your belief that magic exists suggests there's something missing in your life."

"Such as?"

"You could be using this fantasy to give you a system to operate in. Almost like a belief system or a faith. The magic creates a skeleton to hang everything else on."

"Faith? You're asking me to believe in a higher being?"

"Or simply recognize you're part of something bigger. It doesn't have to be a god."

"It's not that. My games are important to me, and I enjoy my job, but these dreams I have are so intense. And the visions..." I shook my head. It was hard to describe what I'd seen and experienced. It was something other. Something not normal. Something magical.

"Have they changed? You mentioned seeing flashes of light and thought you were being watched, but there's never anyone there."

"It's the same, although they're getting more frequent."

"You've not added any medication or tried natural remedies? Some of the CBD drops they sell are strong. They alter perception if you take enough of them."

"Nothing like that. I've been trying the relaxation techniques you suggested and the meditation, but they make no difference."

"It can take a while. Give it another month. If that doesn't work, I'll suggest a prescription medication."

"I don't want pills to mask the symptoms. I need to know what this is."

"You want the visions and the feeling of being watched to disappear, don't you?"

"Sure. It's creepy thinking someone is following you. The weird light flashes and strange smells I can handle."

"Medication can help if this turns out to be a chemical imbalance. We have excellent on-site doctors who'll make a tailored recommendation. Therapy and the appropriate medication will change everything."

"Sounds great."

Tom smiled. "It's a sensible course of action. But with your intense work schedule, you must factor in time to relax. Overwork is a killer. In Japan, they call it karoshi. It translates into overwork death."

"I have no plans to die at my desk."

Tom tapped his pen on the pad resting on his knee. "If you cut back your hours to a more regular forty or fifty hours a week, your problems could go away. Why don't we focus on that?"

"And do what? My work is my life."

"Remember karoshi."

Maybe Tom thought he was being impressive with his Japanese knowledge, but I was losing patience.

"Will your work be there on your deathbed? Do you think it'll say goodbye and pat you on the head because you did such a good job?" Tom shook his head. "If you left your job for a few months, you wouldn't be missed. I hate to be harsh, but everyone is replaceable, no matter what incredible magical system you dream up."

"You've never played the Forests of Avalon." My games rocked the gaming community. I'd had three in the top ten charts for almost a year.

Tom set down his pen. "Your work has overtaken your life, and you're blurring reality with fantasy. It's not the first time I've seen cases like this. Guys get obsessed with a project, and that's all they think about. We get single-minded. All or nothing. It haunts us day and night."

"You get like this?"

"No, but I focus hard on having a solid balance in my life."

Of course, Tom hadn't gotten into therapy to sort out his own messed up head. Wasn't that why all people became shrinks? "What happens to the guys who don't get their Zen on and find balance?"

"They burn out. Some lose their edge or simply can't get out of bed. We're human beings with an operating system not meant for this twenty-four-hour culture and obsession with screen time. If we work too hard and put ourselves through too much stress for too long, something will break. Maybe not physically, but in here." He tapped the side of his head.

I didn't like to agree with Tom, but I could try harder. "I'll keep trying the meditation."

"Excellent. I'll also send you a link to some cognitive behavioral therapy. It's a proven method to change the way you think about things. It's been effective for all addictions."

"I don't have an addiction."

Tom tapped away on the tablet he'd picked up. "I'm going to disagree with you. You refuse to cut back on your working hours. You dream about something that doesn't exist, and you're having visual hallucinations. All signs you have work to do. Keep up with the meditation, do the cognitive behavioral therapy, and speak to your employer about reducing your hours. If they value you, they'll make it happen. Oh, and cut back on the caffeine." He looked at the empty takeout mug I'd brought in with me.

"I only have a few cups a day."

"Caffeine overstimulates the adrenals. Combine that with stress and long hours, and you could be in real trouble." He checked the time. "That's our hour up. I'll book you in for the same time next week."

"Sure. Thanks. See you then." It was an effort to pull myself out of the chair and walk into the reception area. No amount of talking would help, but I had to find something that would work. Maybe taking a few minutes to myself and clearing my head would help, but it wouldn't stop the visions.

I checked in at the reception desk with Maggie and pulled out my wallet. "What do I owe you?"

"Same as always. All fixed?" Her big smile lit up her dark eyes behind cat's eye glasses.

"Almost. I'll be back next week, though, just to make sure nothing has shaken loose and needs a repair."

"Perfect. I've already had your next appointment through from Doctor Saunders." Maggie pressed my card against the payment screen. "You had a late session. Is Mrs. Drake picking you up?"

"No, I'm walking home. It's near here."

"I'm sure she'll have made you a nice dinner. You can relax together." Maggie studied the card reader.

I rubbed the back of my neck. "There is no Mrs. Drake. I'll pick up takeout. There's a decent Thai place close by."

Maggie's eyes widened, and her fingers brushed mine as she passed me my card. "I don't like to think of you going home alone. Your girlfriend will be there, won't she?"

I stepped away from the desk, shoving my card into my wallet. "Nope."

Her tongue darted out. "This won't sound professional, but do you mind me asking if you're single?"

"I don't mind. And I am. Work keeps me busy." There was something else that kept me from dating, though. Or rather, someone else.

"Oh, I'm the same. Tom is a slave driver. I don't mind, though. I like this job. It's good to help people. I mean, not that you need help. You seem fine."

"I appreciate that, but I wouldn't be coming to therapy if I was fine."

Her cheeks flushed. "Of course. What I meant was we have all kinds of people who come for therapy. And I'm not breaking confidentiality by saying this, but some of them are messed up. They've been coming for years to get their heads right. Others simply need a few sessions to figure things out."

"You think I fit the last category?"

"I hope so. Because when you've finished your treatment, I'd love to take you for a coffee."

"Oh! Um... thanks. Tom told me I can't drink coffee."

She giggled. "Or tea, beer, water. Whatever you like. Dating patients isn't allowed, but once you're done, we could meet anytime. Do anything."

"That's sweet of you, Maggie, but I'm not dating right now. I'm... focusing on myself." It was a lame comment, but I really was making my health a priority.

Her mouth twisted to the side. "Take my number. When you feel ready, let's talk. No pressure."

Maggie was pretty and friendly, but she wasn't what I was looking for, and I didn't want to give her any false hope that I'd call. "You seem like a great lady, but I'm not the guy for you."

"Maybe you are. You just don't know it yet." She held her phone out.

"Do you like role play?"

"What are we talking? A French maid outfit?"

"No! Witches and wizards. Magic. Dragons. Tom believes I prefer fake worlds to real ones."

"Oh! That kind of role play." Her face went scarlet. "Board games?"

"Online games. I don't see you as the kind of girl who'd happily sit by my side for hours while I play

Dungeons and Dragons or work on coding for the latest glitch in a game. That's what I do all day, every day. It makes me happy."

"You must go out to eat. Or we could go for a drink. Anything you like. It could get your mind back in the real world."

I arched an eyebrow. "You haven't been reading my file, have you?"

"No! I'd never do that. I'd lose my job. But the way you talk, it made me wonder if you need more fun in your life."

"I have fun. I sometimes even play laser quest."

Her smile faltered, and she lowered her phone. "You know where I am if you change your mind."

"I'm flattered, Maggie. Thanks again, but now's a bad time for me." I dashed out of the office.

Maggie would probably make the perfect girlfriend. She was cute, had a good job, and didn't seem complicated. But there was only one woman I wanted, and she lived in my fantasies. I saw her in my dreams all the time. She smelled like rain and sometimes garlic bread. I couldn't get her out of my thoughts, and the option of dating anyone else wasn't there. I'd met no one in real life who came close to her. Unfortunately, until I did, dating was out of the question.

I welcomed the cool evening air as I stepped outside. It had just gone nine in the evening. Tom usually shut at eight, but this was the only time I could get off work, and I'd paid double for the session, so he could hardly complain.

Tom thought I was just another loser nerd, obsessed with games and nothing else. And maybe that was a problem for some but not me. I got his point about working too hard, though. What else did I have? No wife, no girlfriend, or any family left. Not even a cat. All my friendships were online.

And the gaming community was amazing. No one mocked me when I talked about magic systems or fighting evil with spells and potions. They encouraged me. My tribe of questing geeks welcomed me in.

I didn't have a family waiting for me at home, but when I opened my computer and logged on, I had my perfect found family there. A band of messy, too smart for their own good misfits, who made their own world, one we fit in so much better than this cold, clinical reality.

While I waited at the lights until it was safe to cross the road, my phone buzzed with an incoming message. I pulled it out.

*New game starts in thirty minutes. You in?*

It was Lord Storm Thrower, a regular gaming buddy. He was loud, obnoxious, and his avatar had an eight-pack and glowing green eyes.

*I'll be there. What's the mission?*

*Usual dark witch scum wanting to take over and destroy the world. Exclusive game, only four of us. Don't be late.*

*See you soon.* I signed off with the initials FF. We all had gaming names, and I'd picked Fire Fang. My avatar was a seven foot half-man, half-werewolf with huge teeth. I breathed fire and growled so loud the ground shook.

It was a better look than my human form. I worked out and didn't slob out too much on the junk food, but how amazing would it be to breathe actual fire and make the ground tremble under my paws?

I strode across the road. The real world could suck it. There was somewhere else and someone else I much preferred to be.

# Chapter 2

There she was. My perfect woman. She was tall and slender and strode around with so much confidence, but I could tell she was vulnerable. I called her Winter. She didn't smile much, but her focus was always on helping those who needed it. She was a bringer of justice. Sometimes, that justice was dealt out harshly with incredible blasts of power. Winter protected the underdog and made sure the bad guys never got away with it.

She also controlled the weather. She could slam lightning bolts into her enemy with a slash of her hands. Winter was magnificent. And she was the only woman I was interested in. Every time I dreamed about her, she felt so real.

Winter was smart, determined, and resourceful. Her only flaw was her terrible table manners. I mean, she could stuff a whole giant muffin in her mouth. She also had a wicked sharp, stubborn streak, which I got off on.

My eyes flickered open, and the dream slowly faded, but Winter never completely disappeared. She spent her days and nights with me, surrounded by her magical friends in a cute little village. It was a place brimming with magic and power. Ancient ley lines flickered beneath the ground, ensuring those who lived there remained powerful. The village attracted attention, though, and Winter was always battling some lowlife who wanted a piece of that power.

With reluctance, I pushed away the dream. I checked the time. It had just gone five in the morning, and I needed to grab a coffee and hit the gym before work.

I liked to be in by six-thirty. Stardust Industries wasn't your average nine-to-five place. Run by billionaire eccentric Gideon Masters, he offered incredible benefits in exchange for complete devotion. When you worked on a new project, you didn't stop until it was done. He lived by that philosophy, often sleeping in the office and working through the night with international clients to get deals done.

I rolled out of bed and into the bathroom, checking my reflection in the mirror. Gideon hired the best and those prepared to put in the hours to make sure his billions kept growing. I had no objection to that. In a few years, if I wanted, I'd have enough money to retire.

But I couldn't see it happening. I'd start a gaming business or search for a place like the village in my dreams. I could move there and spend my days hunting for magic.

Gym clothes on, I headed into the kitchen.

Red glitter covered the countertop. I placed my finger on the surface and slid it back. The glitter transferred to my skin. Where had that come from?

I lived alone, and only my cleaner had a set of keys. She wouldn't leave red glitter after cleaning. Besides, she wasn't due for two days.

I checked the bedroom, bathroom, and lounge. The kitchen countertop was the only place covered in glitter. But why, and who had left it there?

I grabbed a baseball bat from the closet in the hallway and crept around, chills rioting down my spine. Had someone broken in to leave red glitter? Why do that? I checked behind every door, in all the closets, under the bed, and investigated the windows to see if anyone had broken in. There was no one there. The place was empty and the windows locked.

The red glitter hadn't been there last night. Someone must have put it there. I wasn't a red glitter kind of guy, so I didn't have a stash of spray on glitter I'd forgotten I'd used.

Was this a vision? I clicked some pictures on my phone and scanned through them. The glitter was visible. I sent them to Lord Storm Thrower.

*What do you see in these pictures?*

It went through but didn't get read. He was probably sleeping after our mammoth gaming session last night.

My phone beeped, and I jumped. It wasn't Lord Storm Thrower but an alert I'd be late for work if I didn't hustle.

I grabbed a cloth, swept the glitter into the trash, grabbed my gym bag and last night's takeout bag, and headed outside.

Maybe the glitter had been on the takeout bag. I'd been in a rush, so I didn't miss the start of the gaming session, but that was a lot of glitter to miss. And why would the restaurant cover its takeout bags in glitter?

I checked the bag before tossing it. No glitter. Maybe it would remain a mystery.

I smirked as I jogged to the gym. Or maybe it was magic.

Once my workout was done, I had a five-minute shower, changed into jeans and a sweater, and headed into work.

Stardust Industries dominated a huge corner of the technology district of Avonsville. It was an imposing, glass fronted building with fifteen floors. The place was owned by Gideon, with different divisions operating out of each floor. Gideon wasn't just a gaming entrepreneur; he was an early adopter for space travel and colonization of other planets. He invested his billions into expanding the possibilities available to people, not only in real life, but through the games he commissioned.

Two floors were dedicated to gaming project development. And I spent most of my time in the open plan area on the fourteenth floor.

I used my badge to sign in at reception, allowed my fingerprints to be scanned, then headed to the elevator. Gaming was big business, and people stole concepts all the time, so security was tight. You couldn't wander in off the street and poke about. Well, you could try, but armed security would show you the exit fast.

I used my key card to access the elevator and was soon upstairs, stepping out into a white office. It had been designed in zones, and the white walls were the only plain thing. Each floor had different zones, but wherever you were, there was always the sense of the outdoors. Gideon believed plants inspired creativity, so there was AstroTurf carpeting, real vines, a living tree growing through the center of the building, and wooden hobbit holes for when you needed alone time to think all things magical. At least, that's what I used them for.

I wasn't the first to arrive. Jed and Tony were at their desks and looked like they'd been there all night if the bleary eyes and empty cups were anything to go by. Rhonda and Tegan were also there, chatting by the drinks machine.

Everything was custom-made and designed to provide everything we needed without leaving the building. We even had an on-site gym downstairs, but I preferred to use one away from here. After all, Tom said I needed a life outside of work.

"How's it going?" Jed raised a hand in greeting. We were similar in looks, with the same scruffy dark hair and beard, but he was shorter than me and had fewer tattoos.

"Good. Had an epic quest last night with Lord Storm Thrower."

"What! And you left me out again? That guy is a pig. You should have let me know and I'd have joined."

"It was invite only, and it wasn't my invitation to give out." I shrugged off my backpack, poured a mug of Saint Helena coffee, and settled at my desk, flicking on the three large screens around me.

"Lord Storm Thrower is a jerk. I keep asking him to let me in on a mission. He keeps telling me I'm

not ready. I'm a young Jedi and have much to learn."
Jed snorted. "I've got as much experience as you."

I chuckled as I fired up my systems and checked my messages. "Don't take it personally. He did that to me for a while. It was only when I threatened to start my own mission and defeat him by hacking a back door into his game that he let me in. He's testing you. He wants to see how dedicated you are to joining the elite team."

"You think?"

"You couldn't hack Lord Storm Thrower's game. The guy's a crazy genius," Tony said.

"I could if I wanted. His games aren't that good. How'd you do it?" Jed leaned forward in his seat.

"I can't let you in on my secrets. And you wouldn't have had fun last night. We didn't finish till three in the morning," I said.

"What was the mission?" Tony grinned as he grabbed his own mug of coffee.

I always got a thrill talking game tactics with my friends. "We had to breach Titan Max. There were four of us against five other teams."

"Awesome. Did you claim the champion title?"

Jed groaned. "Stop! This is causing me physical pain. I could have helped. My avatar is strong, fast, and versatile."

"And prefers splatting opponents rather than negotiating with them," Tony said.

"True. And we already had a splatter orc on the team. Better luck next time," I said.

"Like I care. Sounds boring." Jed's expression told me he thought it was exactly the opposite.

"I'll see if I can get you an invitation next time." I opened the tricky chunk of coding I'd been working on and scanned through it. There was a glitch somewhere, but I'd yet to work it out.

"Hey, Noah." Tegan stopped by my desk, her fingers teasing her pink hair. She was whip smart and incredible at creating single expansive game play. She was new to the team and had been here three months but was making a name for herself.

"How's the Siren's Call going?" I said.

"Sticky. I wanted your advice about a coding problem."

Jed chuckled and nudged Tony.

I glared at him. "Sure. What do you need?"

"I see you're busy. We could work on it while we eat lunch. It's sushi day. Brain food for super geeks."

"Gross. Slimy fish and sweet rice. I'm happier when it's pizza day," Jed said.

"Tegan wasn't inviting you." I played with the mouse on my desk, bringing up an image of an avatar I'd been working on.

"Who's that?" Tegan looked at my screen. "She's cute."

"Oh, just a design I've been messing around with." Warmth spread from the center of my chest as I studied the image of Winter I'd worked on ever since she entered my dreams.

"I can guarantee you're looking at his dream woman," Jed said. "If she's got pale skin and dark hair, that's his secret girlfriend."

"You have a girlfriend?" Tegan said.

"No! I mean, I'm not dating right now. Wint — this isn't my girlfriend." My warning glare told Jed to shut it, but he was a guy with poor social awareness. Or maybe he was just a jerk. "You know what it's like. You get an idea and it has to come out."

Tegan leaned closer to the screen. "She's great. You should include her in your next game. She could even be a main character."

"I'm considering it."

"She looks magical. Sort of witchy. A perfect fit. Have you settled on a title for the game yet? Everyone keeps guessing what it could be," Tegan said.

"It's too early to have a name."

"It's not. Noah's scared to name his baby, in case it comes out ugly and covered in fur," Jed said.

"I'm not scared. But what if people hate the name I pick?" I said. "Remember the game Fable Arch Rogue Team?"

Tony snort laughed. "FART! How could we forget?"

"No one could hate your work." Tegan ignored Jed and Tony as they made gross noises by squashing their hands under their armpits. "And I've played the early design during beta testing. It's amazing. Those witches were scary. Your dream woman should be in there, too. You must have a name for her."

"Not yet." I clicked off the screen. "Let's grab that lunch and we can talk about the kinks."

Tegan grinned at me. Her gaze went to my shoulder, and she leaned forward and brushed it. "What's with the glitter on your clothes?"

"From his hot date last night," Jed said. "A burlesque dancer from Peppermint Screams."

I checked my shoulder. There was glitter on my clothes. "Weird. I've no clue where it's coming from. Definitely not from a hot date. I found some in my apartment this morning, too."

Tegan rubbed it between her fingers before blowing it off. "I'll see you later."

"Sure. Later." I kept scrubbing at the glitter.

"She's seriously into you," Jed said, the second Tegan was out of earshot.

"Then I feel sorry for her," I said. "Who wants to be stuck with one of us?"

"Tegan's cool. And she's into gaming. I know she does D&D. You should take her out."

"I'm not looking for anyone."

"What's the worst that could happen? You take a cute girl out and talk about gaming all night."

"I don't want to give her the wrong idea." I kept inspecting the glitter. Under the office lights, it shimmered. And it wouldn't budge, no matter how much I rubbed.

"Hey! Focus. Tegan could be good for you. Even if she isn't the witch of your dreams, you could still have fun with her," Jed said.

I shook my head. "I'm getting more coffee."

"Bring me some," Tony said.

I was heading over to grab coffee when I heard my name. I slowed and tilted my head.

"I've tried several times, but unless I'm carrying a sword and spinning magic around my head, Noah doesn't notice me."

That was Cindy Sable who worked on the reception desk.

"He's gorgeous. That's the frustrating thing. He's the perfect guy, looks wise, and he has no idea. He looks like a seedy pirate who'd ravish you in the bedroom then protect you from the bad guys." That was Emilie. She'd asked me out a few times, but I'd always declined. She was a man eater, and I didn't like getting bitten.

"He's such a sweetheart," Cindy said.

"I love he gets so embarrassed when anyone flirts with him."

I didn't! Maybe I wasn't some smooth talking jerk with dozens of lines, but I knew how to talk to women. I just didn't do it all that often when out socially.

"If any other guy looked like him, they'd be bedding women all over the place. It's adorable Noah doesn't do that," Emilie said. "But neither of us stand a chance. He's waiting for his perfect woman. I overheard him talking about her to Jed and Tony."

"Who is she? I'll find her then kill her and give myself a chance."

"Don't be weird." Emilie chuckled. "Unless you decide to go into a game and destroy her with a spell, there's nothing you can do. According to Jed, she's not real. Noah's dream woman lives in his head."

"What!" Cindy made a noise of disgust. "Such a waste. All those muscles and brooding dark looks, and the guy hasn't got a clue. He's such a socially awkward hot mess. It's kind of sexy."

"All he needs is a good woman to fix him."

"You want to be that good woman?"

"Sure. So do you. So does every warm-blooded woman in this office. But Noah Drake's head will only turn if you zap him in the butt with a spell and cover him in a love potion."

I gripped my mug, my teeth grinding. No one enjoyed being gossiped about. I had flaws. It was why I was in therapy, but the gossiping needed to end. I pulled back my shoulders, turned the corner, and walked straight into a guy carrying a tray of donuts.

# Chapter 3

My hands shot out to catch the donuts. A spark of electricity shot from my fingers and hit them, covering them in a red shimmer. They slowed and floated in the air.

I blinked, not believing what I was seeing. Donuts didn't float, and people didn't fire electric sparks out of their hands.

I grabbed the tray and thrust it under the sugary treats, catching most of them, although I lost a few when they stopped floating and hit the floor.

"You idiot!"

My gaze darted up, and horror rose in me like a stepped-on dragon. It was Sylvester the Sneak. He was Gideon's best buddy and always sided with him, no matter what he said or did. He was also a ruthless manipulator who'd gotten where he was by being Gideon's yes-man.

Sylvester was infamous for snooping and listening into private conversations to see if anyone said anything bad about Gideon or the company. If he learned you were gossiping, you were fired.

"Sorry. I didn't see you. I was coming to talk to..." My gaze flicked to Emilie and Cindy, who were staring at us in silence. "I was in a hurry."

"Pay attention, you jerk. If you're this sloppy around the office, who knows what mess you'll make of the coding in your fancy new game." Sylvester flipped a chunk of donut off his shoe, leaving behind a greasy mark on the polished surface.

"Why were you lurking around the corner? I didn't see you."

"I wasn't lurking! Gideon wanted to treat everyone, so he sent me for cake." Sylvester scraped ineffectively at a grease mark on his Ralph Lauren shirt. "And you're in trouble."

"I already said sorry for bumping into you."

"Not that. The last piece of coding you sent over was glitchy."

"It was triple checked. It's fine."

"It's flawed. And where's the test run of the latest issue of that weird witch game you keep obsessing over? Gideon wanted it yesterday. What's the hold-up?"

"No hold-up. Everything is running on time. I have the deadlines in my calendar." I grabbed a sponge from the sink and offered it to Sylvester. He ignored it.

"He wants it immediately."

"Is that his order or yours? If I rush, there'll definitely be coding mistakes." And Sylvester would love that. He took pleasure in seeing other people fail because it made him look like Mr. Perfect.

Sylvester's cold blue bulging eyes narrowed. "Just get on with it. And you owe me a new shirt."

I raised a hand. There was no point in arguing with Sylvester, and I had slammed into him because I was angry at being gossiped about and not paying attention. "Send me the bill. You know I'm good for it."

"I do. I've seen your wage slip. You gamers earn too much."

"If you think I'm paid too much, speak to Gideon. There are other companies that will use my skills. They might even pay better."

Sylvester smirked. "You'll never leave. You've got it too good here. Gideon lets you do what you like."

I didn't disagree. The benefits were incredible, but burnout was real in this industry. I had a plan, though, and it didn't involve staying here the rest of my life and being hassled by Sylvester.

"Would you like a cloth?" Emilie stepped forward, holding out a damp cloth for Sylvester.

"Waste of time. This shirt is ruined. And so are those donuts. You owe me for those, too." Sylvester stomped away, muttering to himself and dabbing at his shirt.

I looked at the tray. I'd saved most of the donuts, apart from the ones that hit Sylvester and a couple that escaped by... well, I didn't know what to call it. Had they floated away?

"Don't worry about Sylvester." Emilie placed a hand on my arm. "You know how he always insists on being impeccably dressed."

"It's to make up for his appalling manners," Cindy whispered, peeking around to make sure no one was listening to her badmouthing the boss's right-hand man.

"After I got over the shock of you walking into him, I was trying not to laugh. He looked so angry," Emilie said, a smile playing on her lips.

"You both saw what happened, didn't you?" I said.

"Of course. We were right here," Cindy said. "Come sit with us. You need a break after dealing with Sylvester."

I was still focused on the donuts. "And you saw me catch these?"

"You have lightning fast reflexes," Cindy said. "So impressive."

"That was all you saw?"

"That was it. One second, the donuts were flying, and the next you had them on the tray. Did I miss something?" Cindy glanced at Emilie, and they both shrugged.

"How did I catch them?"

The ladies exchanged a puzzled glance. "With the tray. You snatched it from Sylvester."

"I mean, how did I do that?"

"Well, you're a big, strong guy. Good reflexes?" Emilie's eyes lit with amusement.

I wasn't looking for flattery. I was looking for the answer to how these donuts floated. "What about the spark?"

"Um... what spark?" Emilie said.

"I saw... I thought I saw something electrical. Like a discharge of power."

"From something in the kitchen?" Emilie looked around.

My mouth twisted to the side. Had these treats floated, or had I experienced a vision in front of other people? They usually happened when I was alone, but maybe my issue was getting worse.

"I was impressed by how you kept your cool with Sylvester," Emilie said. "He loves to rile people."

"He does it because he's bored," Cindy said. "I'm not even sure what his job is. Intimidator? Problem causer? I don't know why Gideon keeps him around."

"They went to Eton together. They're childhood friends." I picked up a donut and turned it over. It looked like your average deep-fried treat with a layer of icing and a thick cream filling. Your basic heart attack in cake form.

"They look delicious," Cindy said. "I'll make you a coffee, and we can all have one."

"Good idea. Join us." Emilie gestured at the table.

I followed them into the kitchenette area, all plans to let them know what I thought about their gossiping forgotten.

Cindy held out a coffee for me. "Just how you like it. Strong and black with a dash of sugar."

"Thanks. The donuts, though." I lifted the tray.

"I'll have the pink one." Emilie chose a donut.

Cindy set my drink on the table. She looked at Emilie again and gave another little shrug.

"This will sound strange, but did you see these donuts floating? I went to catch them and... something happened. They slowed down."

Unsurprisingly, both ladies looked at me as if I'd suggested I didn't have all my faculties.

"You think you saw them floating?" Emilie said. Her lips quirked up. "Are you teasing us?"

"I did. At least, I thought I did." I set the tray of donuts on the counter, not able to take my eyes off them.

"It's the stress. It gets to all of us working here. And you splatted Sylvester with several donuts. That's enough to cause heart palpitations," Cindy said. "The look on his face was priceless, though. He only got them because Gideon mentioned he had a craving this morning."

I remained standing, despite them sitting at the table with their drinks and donuts. This felt weird. It would have taken less than two seconds for those cakes to hit the floor, but I'd grabbed the tray from Sylvester and positioned it so I caught most of them. It was a physical impossibility.

Unless... Unless they really had floated. And where had that spark come from? I didn't wear a watch or a fitness tracker, so it wasn't that malfunctioning. The spark had come out of my hand.

I inspected my palm, but there was no burn or red mark, although the skin tingled.

"Don't look so worried," Emilie said. "Sylvester will never convince Gideon to get rid of you. You're an asset. Everyone knows you're keeping this place going and making Gideon insanely wealthy."

"That's nice of you to say." I pulled out a chair but couldn't settle.

"Sylvester will find someone else to pick on by the afternoon," Cindy said. "Keep your head down, give Gideon something juicy for the new game, and whatever Sylvester says about you, he won't listen. He's got more sense than to get rid of his golden boy."

"Golden man. You're a golden man. He's not a boy. I mean... well, you know what I mean. All man." Emilie's cheeks flushed pink, and she stuffed a chunk of donut into her mouth.

"Err... thanks. It's a team effort. I'm not creating this new game on my own. That would be impossible."

"It was your concept," Cindy said. "And everyone thinks it's brilliant."

I lifted another donut and turned it over. "This doesn't make sense."

"They taste good," Cindy said. "Sylvester went to that expensive boutique bakery on the corner. They charge three times the price of anywhere else, but you can taste the quality."

Maybe it was the lack of sleep making me think and see strange things. I'd only had a few hours after my mammoth gaming session with Lord Storm Thrower. Could I have imagined donuts floating?

"Are you okay?" Cindy said. "You've gone pale. Maybe eat a donut. Sugar is good for shock."

"And even if it's not, a treat will make you feel better," Emilie said.

I rubbed my forehead. I didn't feel so good. I had a low level headache thumping behind my eyes, and my stomach grumbled, but it wasn't from hunger. It felt like I'd eaten something bad and it was coming back for a vicious revenge attack.

"If you're still stressed at the end of the day, I know a great place that does incredible massages," Emilie said. "Deep tissue. You walk out of there feeling lighter than air. I recommend them. Mention my name and you'll get a discount."

"Are you sure you saw nothing strange going on with these donuts?" I said.

Emilie's smile faded. "Noah, this isn't some computer game. Donuts don't behave strangely. You were just quick at catching them. It's not as if you used a magic spell to make sure they didn't hit the floor."

"I know how much you want it to be, but magic isn't real." Cindy's bottom lip jutted out, and she made little noises of sympathy at me.

"Yeah, sure, I know that. It's just..." I couldn't explain this. Well, there was one explanation. My head was too far gone, and I'd started my epic breakdown at work. What a way to go. Sylvester would delight in calling an ambulance and having me taken away for an assessment.

"We should get back to work." Cindy's expression suggested I'd disappointed her, but I was only trying to get to the truth, even if that made me look strange.

"Let me know if you want the details of that masseuse. And the salon does joint sessions too, so we could go together," Emilie said.

I nodded but couldn't muster enthusiasm for getting rubbed down by a stranger, especially not with gossipy Emilie watching.

After a few seconds of uncomfortable hovering, Cindy nudged Emilie. "We're wasting our time. Let's go."

They left me in the kitchenette with the odd donuts and a throbbing head. The second they were gone, I grabbed a donut and tossed it in the air. I thrust out my hands. The donut hit the tiled floor.

I focused and tried with another. I threw it higher and willed it to slow. It did the same thing as the first one.

"Come on, I know what I saw. Something made these donuts float." It wasn't some shift in the gravitational pull that had affected their motion. What if... what if I'd made them float?

Yeah, perfect solution. No one else had seen them floating, so it was my eyes messing with me.

Three more thrown donuts later and one messy floor, and I was seriously doubting myself and my sanity.

Jed poked his head around the door. "Um... are you leaving any of those donuts unmolested for the rest of us? Several people have come over to tell me you're donut tossing. What have those delicious slabs of greasy joy ever done to you?"

My face grew warm, and I grabbed the fallen donuts and put them in the trash. "I was testing a theory."

"A theory that only you get to play with the donuts?" Jed walked in and grabbed a chocolate cream filled donut that hadn't been splatted.

"No. I mean, I don't know what I'm doing." I scraped a hand through my hair.

"Emilie said you were distracted by something. She also said you almost picked a fight with Sylvester. Never a good move this early in the day.

He'll be on your back for hours until he thinks he's gotten revenge."

"I didn't pick the fight." I nudged the leftover donuts at him. "I'm done with these. You can hand them out if you like."

"My man!" Jed grinned, stuff the donut into his mouth, grabbed the tray, and left the room.

I must have imagined it, or it was a trick of the light. And maybe Cindy and Emilie were right, and I just had fast reflexes. But the spark, and that weird feeling...

I grabbed an apple someone had left on the countertop and tried one last time. It hit the floor just like all the donuts and rolled away.

A piercing head pain had me grimacing and grabbing for something to hold on to. I was about to pass out as the agony splintered through my brain. Accompanying the pain was an ache in my gut. This was bad. It felt like I was about to explode.

Gripping my head and stomach, I raced to the washroom. I was grateful it was empty as I dashed inside and secured the door behind me.

I leaned over the sink, black dots sparking in my vision. I needed to get on the floor before I passed out and smashed my head on the porcelain.

I took several deep breaths to stay conscious. My gut spasmed, and I let out an enormous burp. A jet of flames blasted out of my mouth and set fire to a stack of toilet paper.

# Chapter 4

The toilet paper ignited, and flames licked around the stack and hit the ceiling. I stared at the flames and then at my face in the mirror. I'd expected to see blisters and burns on my lips, but there was nothing. My throat felt scratchy but not destroyed, which it should have been, because freaking flames had come out of my mouth.

I turned on the cold water, filled my hands with it, and threw it at the flames. But it was too little, too late, and they were out of control. The ceiling was alight, and the hand dryer next to the towels was melting.

I kept throwing more and more water. Then an alarm beeped overhead, and the sprinklers activated.

The flames were doused, leaving me soaked, and a soggy, blackened mess in one corner where the toilet paper had been.

I looked in the mirror again. My eyes were wide and my face pale. I poked out my tongue and peered down my throat. How had this happened? People didn't belch fire, or if they did, it only ever happened in one of my online games. My avatar, Fire Fang, loved fire breathing, but this was real life.

The pain in my head and stomach faded, but I still felt lousy and was certain I'd do it again if I wasn't careful. But how could I be careful about breathing fire when it was impossible to do?

Floating donuts, sparking hands, and fire breathing? Three huge ticks in the *I'm losing my mind* quiz on the mental health assessment scale. I should bump up my next session with Tom before I was sectioned.

The washroom door slammed open, and Jed looked in. "I thought I saw you head this way. Oh, the fire was in here? Wait! Did you start it?"

Heat flushed up my neck and onto my cheeks. "It was an accident."

"You're in so much trouble. All the equipment's soaked. Come on, we have to evacuate the building. The fire marshal is chasing us out."

I looked at the mess then followed Jed. We had to take the stairs because the elevator was out of action.

Jed nudged me. "I won't say anything about you being a devious fire starter."

"I don't know what happened," I whispered.

"How did you do it?"

I considered Jed a buddy, but he couldn't keep a secret to save his life, and there was no way he'd believe flames had come out of my mouth. "I... lit a match. Dropped it by accident."

"Okay. Why do that?"

"I don't know. I just did."

"Weirdo. I don't think anyone else saw you go into the washroom. If you keep quiet, you might get away with it. Or you can blame someone else. Blame Sylvester. He's always sneaking off for a smoke in the stalls. It's such a gross habit. You can smell the smoke on him."

"It was my fault. I need to tell Gideon what happened."

"You sure? You've cost him a serious amount of money. The guy likes you, but you're pushing your luck. He could fire you over this."

"Then he fires me. I'm not letting anyone else take the blame for my mistake."

Jed gave me a friendly punch on the arm. "I'll buy you a drink at your leaving party."

We reached the bottom of the stairs and headed outside with everyone else to the assembly point.

I looked around for Gideon and discovered him talking to Sylvester. Gideon looked furious, and Sylvester was scurrying around him, nodding and gesturing at the building.

"I'd better get this over with," I said to Jed.

He patted me on the back. "I'll be here to clean up the body parts once Gideon has ripped you apart."

"You're a good friend." I strode over to Gideon. He was a tall, broad shouldered guy in his mid-forties, with thick dark hair and matching eyebrows. He was the kind of guy people looked at when he walked into a crowded room. He had that air of power and confidence. It got him noticed.

"Gideon, I need to talk to you," I said.

He glanced my way and smiled. "Noah! I hope this incident won't mess with your creative urges. I'm looking forward to testing the new game."

"It won't be a problem. And I can make up for the lost time. But it's not that. I started the fire."

Sylvester sucked in a breath then a sly smile spread across his face. "You're a walking disaster. I've already told Gideon what you did to me this morning. I'm still not sure it was an accident."

Gideon's gaze went to the building. "Why start a fire?"

"It wasn't deliberate. I wasn't feeling great, so went to the washroom. I... lit a match and dropped it in the pile of toilet rolls. The next thing I knew, they'd gone up in flames. I tried to put it out, but then the sprinkler system activated. I'm so sorry."

"You're not a child. Grown men don't play with matches because they're not feeling well," Sylvester said. "The computers are destroyed, working hours lost, and people's days ruined. The office might have to be shut for weeks to get everything back in place."

Gideon was still staring at the building. "It was only our floor affected. Much damage in the washroom?"

"No. And I'll pay for the repairs."

"And replace all the computers, I suppose?" Sylvester said.

Gideon raised a hand. "That won't be necessary. I was thinking about making over that floor. And some of those computers are a year old. Everyone is due an upgrade. With my expansion plans, we need the most sophisticated equipment out there. Noah,

I was going to talk to you about specifications for the upgrades."

Sylvester opened his mouth to say something but then snapped his jaw shut. Hatred burned in his eyes, and it was directed at me.

"You were?" I said.

"You're the best we've got in game design. You know the equipment needs for the team better than anyone. Forget the fire. Let's call it fate nudging me in the right direction. I've been occupied with other ventures and put the renovations on the back burner. Now everything's had a drenching, I can get the plans into action. I should thank you."

"You should?" Sylvester plucked at his soggy shirt.

"Absolutely. Sylvie, when we get inside, pull the file on my renovation plans. I had a meeting with those designers two months ago. That'll have everything you need. Liaise with the usual refurbishment team to get things moving. While the upgrade is happening, everyone can work remotely or use the top floor and share with finance."

I hid a grin. Sylvester loathed the nickname Sylvie almost as much as he loathed me.

"Of course. As soon as it's safe to go inside, I'll get onto that." Sylvester sent me a death stare.

I was so shocked by Gideon's reaction, I didn't know what to say. He shocked me even more when he put an arm around my shoulders and walked me away from Sylvester.

"Noah, I need you focused on the new game. The company made a killing on your last creative. We're still getting rave reviews even after it's been out for eighteen months. And don't think I haven't noticed how high it's stayed in the gaming chart. You've made something as rare as a unicorn. An evergreen fantasy multi-role-playing game. It's genius."

"Thanks. I appreciate that. We all worked hard to get it right."

"You were the lead. You did the hard work. I may not be around often, but I see things. I know how many hours you work here and how dedicated you are to your games. This isn't a job for you. This is your life, isn't it?"

"So my therapist tells me."

He laughed. "Same here. My therapist told me I'd be dead by thirty-five if I kept working so hard. You know what I did? I put in an extra ten hours that week to show him my passions would never kill me."

"Was he impressed?"

"I sacked him. We had different visions for my future." He thumped my shoulder. "But it's not always about burning the midnight oil. You're efficient. You cut waste and focus on what's important. That's what gets the amazing results. And I know you'll do the same again with this latest game."

Since Gideon had moved on from the fire, I was happy never to remind him of it again. "It's early days, but it looks promising. Feedback from the initial trials is shaping it into something incredible."

"Your weird witch game will be a surefire success. Tell me the concept again. I love hearing you talk about it as if it's real. I get the tingles."

I glanced over my shoulder. Sylvester looked about ready to blow a blood vessel. He hated being sidelined by Gideon. "The basic concept remains unchanged. There'll be a multi-level player platform set in a magical village."

"And the characters? The last concept I saw only had basic sketches. You must have come up with more pivotal characters. I need names, faces, something to bring the world to life and get the gamers horny for more."

"They're mainly all in place if you want to start some teaser promos. I still have the side characters to work on. Jed and Tony are taking the lead on them."

"Make sure you get final approval, though. Fill me in on the main characters. All witches?"

"Yes." I never minded talking game designs with Gideon. Here was a guy with serious visionary power. He never mocked or belittled the magical worlds I created. He recognized their value and how the gaming community loved complete, immersive worlds they could lose themselves in for months.

"Go on. Don't keep me waiting," Gideon said.

"Okay. The main character is called Winter. She's a witch who controls the weather. She has immense power but comes with a troubled past. She suffered loss. Her family gone in tragic circumstances, and she feels alone in the world. But she has a strong sense of justice. She hates the underdogs to lose and fights to her last breath to make sure the good guys win."

"I love it. People adore happy endings for the underdog. Is she hot?"

"She's attractive. I'm making her skills shine more than her makeup."

"Any enhancements? The guys love the hot ones."

"They'll love Winter just as she is. There's nothing fake about her. And she's brutally honest."

Gideon laughed. "I get it, no over-inflated lips or busts. That's your style. I respect that. Who else?"

"I need Winter to have a strong band of brothers around her. Well, sisters. A network she can rely on, but she's always protecting them and worrying about them. She wants to keep them safe. The wrong spell can be lethal."

"Makes sense. In multi-player worlds, you have to have those connections. Do you have names for these characters?"

"Not yet. One of them is a troubled witch who's struggling to get her powers to work because of a dark secret in her past. A secret that'll change her life, if it doesn't get her killed. She also has a strong connection to a werewolf. Although he starts out as her enemy."

"Brilliant. A tangled love story. The female players will go crazy about that. Who else?"

"I have this concept for enchanted scarecrows. There's a witch who has the power to raise the dead and imbue life to the scarecrows. They're big and strong and have a killer instinct. She's so successful with creating these armies of scarecrows, she gains notoriety across the world. But she's also suffered loss. A tragedy that traps her in place and makes her doubt herself. She has to go through her own journey to find peace and happiness."

"Another love story? Not too much?"

"Definitely not. There'll be plenty of action, and the addition of the scarecrow armies she controls will add complexity to her missions."

"Any talking familiars? I always see in the reviews that people love those chatty animals."

"Absolutely. All kinds. The usual cat familiars, but I'm thinking a mutant spider. Something that turns into a giant, killer beast with magic. I want to give it a quirky name, though."

"How about Fluffy the spider?"

"Something like that. Something that'll make the gamers smile."

"We'll do plushie merch. Get people going hyper for the talking cats and spiders, so they want cuddly versions, too." Gideon rubbed his hands together. "I want it all. But we still need a name. Every time I talk about this game, I get hassled by the media. The fans, too. You've got to give me something. Words that inspire greatness, make the fans drool, and give the media something to hang their hats on."

I'd puzzled through thousands of names, but none of them were perfect, and I didn't like to share until I was certain.

"The suspense is killing me," Gideon said. "It could just be a working title. I won't hold you to it. But make it good."

"Haven Witch," I said. "I'm not settled on that, but it's the one I like the most."

"Haven Witch." Gideon rolled it around in his mouth several times. "That'll do. And I want you working full time on this. It must be a priority."

"Of course. All the smaller jobs I'm passing to others on the team, and Tegan has been a great asset. There are a couple of glitches I've discovered in some of the old games that are being worked on. I'm keeping an eye on that, too."

"Ignore the old stuff. That's ticking over. Once the building has been cleaned up following your little fire magic experiment, focus on finishing the first iteration. I need to see my Haven witches in action. And their avatars. Send me what you've been working on."

"I will. First thing tomorrow. I've got a gaming meet tonight. We're testing out the new release from Game Drain."

"No. Cancel it. You know the deal. While we work on a new game, that's all you do. You eat, sleep, and breathe Haven Witch."

"I need to check out the competition, though." And I'd been looking forward to hours of mind bending battles with my online buddies.

Gideon's smile morphed into more of a snarl. "You consider the dirge from Game Drain a threat to our excellence?"

"Not really, but it's always worth checking out. They hired this new team from Japan. They're—"

"Irrelevant."

I knew not to go up against Gideon. "Sure, whatever you need. The gaming meet can wait."

"Good man. You always see sense. Get Haven Witch right, and there'll be a big bonus coming your way."

"Sounds good. Haven Witch is my life from now on."

"And with multiple investors offering their millions to be involved, I'll be able to build two new spaceships with the profits. You play your cards right, and you'll get a free trip into space. Go on a real adventure."

"Ah... thanks. But I like my feet on the ground. I've never been into flying. I don't even have a passport."

Gideon spluttered out a laugh. "You don't need a passport to go into space. I'll save you a seat." He clapped me on the shoulder again then inspected his palm. "Red glitter?"

I looked at my shoulder. Even after being drenched by the sprinklers, there was still a layer of sparkling glitter on me.

He rubbed his hands together. "If glitter is your thing, I'm not complaining, but keep it outside of the office. Glitter is for private fun, got it?"

I brushed the glitter, but it refused to move. "Sure. I have no idea where it came from. I keep finding the damn stuff everywhere."

"Someone's idea of a joke?" Gideon patted my arm. "Make Stardust Industries proud. Although do it without the glitter." He marched back to Sylvester.

I was left with a resigned acceptance that I wouldn't be getting much sleep for the next few months, but so long as I was immersed in Haven Witch, I had no problem with that.

# Chapter 5

I jerked my head up, and pain lanced through my neck. I blinked once, twice, three times. This had to be a dream. I scrubbed my eyes and blinked again. I was awake and floating four feet above my desk.

Normal gravity snapped back into existence, and I thumped down onto the desk, knocking the keyboard to the floor and sending papers and notebooks flying. I lay there, my head spinning and my stomach churning from my unexpected wake-up in mid-air. Nothing felt broken, but I was cold and my arms and legs stiff, suggesting I'd been floating for a while.

I'd been... floating? Like the donuts?

I eased off the desk and rubbed the back of my neck to work out the kink. My gaze lifted. Was I just up there? Was this some prank?

My gaze flickered around the silent, empty office I'd temporarily moved to on the top floor of the building. It wouldn't be the first time Jed and Tony had pulled a trick on me, but nothing like this. They'd have needed to use pulleys and ropes to hoist me out of my seat. And how had they managed that without waking me? Unless they'd drugged me, but even those guys had their limits.

I looked around the open plan office again. A glance out a window showed it was just shifting from dusk to dawn. A check of the time confirmed that after eighteen hours of straight working, I must have passed out at around three in the morning.

This wasn't the first time I'd pulled a long stretch in the office. But none of those previous occasions had resulted in me floating above my desk.

I eased into my chair. I stared at the messy desk and then the space above it. Someone had to be doing this to me. If not physically, then they were messing with my head.

Could it be Sylvester? He was spiking my drinks to make me think I was losing my mind? He was a scheming lowlife, but even he had lines he wouldn't cross. But he was also a devious little sneak, and he hated when Gideon favored anyone over him. And after we'd gotten back in the office yesterday, Gideon had spent more than an hour with me, going over the fine details for Haven Witch. I hadn't missed Sylvester glaring at me like I'd stolen his date for the prom.

Was he nasty enough to threaten the reputation of Stardust Industries by taking out their greatest asset? That wasn't a brag. I worked hard to be this good, and I felt fortunate to be here. There were few people who could claim they'd turned their passion into a lucrative career, but I had. I knew my worth, and so did Sylvester, and he was threatened by it.

I reached for my coffee mug. It was one of the few things I hadn't knocked off the desk when I'd crash landed. I stared into the bottom of the mug. Was that a gritty powder in the coffee sludge?

Sylvester hadn't made me any coffee yesterday. He only ever made coffee for Gideon. But I'd been focused on work. He could easily have passed by the desk and slipped something in when I wasn't paying attention.

I gripped my mug. If this wasn't drug induced, then I must be in the middle of a giant hallucination. And what about the fire breathing? And that annoying red glitter that kept turning up everywhere. Speaking of which, there was glitter on my desk. I was so used to seeing it, I almost didn't mind.

I picked up everything I'd knocked on the floor, tossed away a few broken pens, set my keyboard back in place, and tidied the papers.

I took my empty mug into the kitchenette. This needed some serious thinking, and I couldn't do that without a fresh dose of caffeine running through my veins.

After putting the dirty mug in the dishwasher and choosing a fresh one, I glugged down two mugs of water before making my coffee. Sylvester had left at around eight last night, so whatever he'd given me must almost be out of my system.

When he got in this morning, I was confronting him. It had to be him doing this to me. But I needed proof.

I pulled the dirty mug out of the dishwasher, found a paper bag, and placed it inside. If I had to,

I'd go to the police. I'd get them to test the contents in this mug. If Sylvester had been spiking my drink with hallucinogenic drugs, he'd be the one heading for a fall, not me. I wasn't going down because my success threatened some snide guy with issues.

With the semblance of a plan in place, and after brewing more strong coffee, I walked back to my desk. It would be at least two hours before anyone else showed up, and I'd need that time to get my head together. I didn't want more delusions while there were people around. I'd already played the idiot card by trying to make donuts float. And then there was the weird fire breathing I still couldn't explain. There had to be a logical explanation. If not, my fallback option was that magic was real.

I grinned and took a sip of my coffee. I'd always believed in magic when I was younger, and there was still that small boy in my head yelling it was all real, and it wasn't my imagination making up incredible places like Haven Witch.

If only Winter was real. If she was, I'd move heaven and earth to figure out where Haven Witch was and visit. I'd convince her we were perfect for each other. Of course, knowing Winter as I did, she wouldn't accept it. She'd dig in her heels and pretend she didn't need anyone. But she had a soft center, and I'd get her to reveal it to me.

The sound of a door slamming made me jump, and I spun my seat around, spilling hot coffee over my hand. There was no one by the door.

A shiver ran down my spine, and I spun back the other way. There were eyes on me. Someone had been watching me.

I set down my mug and slowly stood. "Who's in here?"

There was only a faint hum of computers in response.

"Jed, Tony? I'm not in the mood for your games."

Neither of them showed their faces.

I walked the length of the office, checking around partitions and posts, but the space was empty. No one had snuck in. But why had a door slammed if no one was here? All the doors operated on a key card system, and you couldn't wander between floors without permission. Each floor had its own security protocols. I couldn't head down to Space Force and ask the guys about their progress on the dual string three-axis magnetometer, just the same as they couldn't ask insider info about the latest coding in Haven Witch.

After double checking the office was empty, I headed to the door and used my key card to get into the corridor. The lights were on eco-mode, so there was a soft pale amber glow lighting the thick, plush gray carpet. I looked either way along the corridor.

What the... At the far end of the corridor was a curvy blonde woman dressed in pink and yellow. I was so surprised, I stood there with my mouth hanging open. Who was she?

She turned, finger waved at me, and vanished out of sight.

Her movement stirred me into action. "Hey! You're not allowed to be on this floor." I gave chase. I knew everyone in the gaming division. We were a tightknit team, and that mysterious blonde wasn't part of the crew. And I didn't recognize her from the finance team, whose space I was sharing. Even if she worked in that division, what was she doing here so early?

I reached the end of the corridor and turned left, heading in the direction she'd gone. She was fast and had made it all the way along the corridor. She turned and looked back at me. She was kind of pretty, with big blue eyes and lots of glossy makeup, but there was something fake about her that made her look more mannequin than human. She waved again and blew me a kiss.

How had security allowed this woman inside? The main desk on the lower level was staffed twenty-four hours a day. Cameras covered the inside and outside of the building, and there were always two guards on duty during the night shift. She couldn't have walked in off the street and gotten this far without someone seeing her.

"Stop! What are you doing here?"

She didn't respond to my question and kept running. I was impressed at her speed, since she wore those crazy high narrow heels that looked like one slip and you'd break an ankle.

A punch of worry slammed into me as I followed her. What if she was a competitor? Stories circulated all the time about rival firms breaking in and stealing raw game data. Then, when you launched a game, they'd claim it was their concept. They'd provide the stolen evidence of initial concept and design and claim a profit share. Most companies paid out to avoid a scandal and a public battle in court.

And anyone with insider knowledge of how gaming companies worked would know this was the perfect time to strike. Stardust Industries had leaked rumors about Haven Witch to excite the fans. Sneak in before the main beta testing goes live, steal the plans, and the thief would make millions.

But why would a thief break in wearing high heels and a pink frilly dress? Gamers could be oddballs, but her behavior suggested she thought this was fun. If she was caught, she'd end up in jail. Corporate espionage was no joking matter.

I was gasping by the time I'd reached the end of the corridor. I was a regular gym goer, but I was into strength training, not cardio, and it showed. The woman was tiring, too, because she was only halfway along the corridor. I should be able to catch her.

There was a sudden haze in the air, and when it cleared, she was floating! Her feet had lifted several inches off the floor.

I took a few steps toward her and scrubbed my eyes. Still floating. I must be having more side effects from those drugs.

She turned, giggled at me, and floated into an open elevator.

I shook myself and raced toward the elevator, but I was half a second too late as the doors closed. I slammed my finger against the button to get it to open, but it glided to the lower level.

I jabbed the button on the second elevator, but every time I punched it, the light went out. Damn thing must be broken.

How was this woman using the elevator? They wouldn't budge unless you scanned your key card. She must have stolen or forged a card. But then there were the fingerprint scanners to get past when she hit reception.

Whoever she was, she knew what she was doing to be able to bypass our security and avoid the guards.

After giving up on the elevator, I headed to the stairs and bounded down them. Being on the fifteenth floor meant we had amazing views, but it wasn't much fun when you needed to get to the reception in a hurry.

I used the banisters to propel myself down without breaking bones. Once the woman got to the lower level, she'd be trapped. Security would see her, and she wouldn't be able to get out the main door. This building had an option to go to full security lockdown with the press of a button, trapping anyone inside. I'd yell at the guard behind the desk to set things in motion, and she'd be caught.

My throat burned as I shoved through the door and into the open plan reception area. I looked around for the woman. No sign of her. I raced to the elevator, but the door was open, and it was empty.

I spun around. Where was she? My eyes widened. She was outside, surrounded by a strange light that seemed to come from her stomach. And she was thirty feet from the building. How?

She turned, as if sensing she was being watched. A wide smile lit her face. The smile was unnaturally big. It showed her teeth and gums. And when she waved at me again, her fingers looked distorted, more like long claws with sharp nail tips.

"Mr. Drake! Is something the matter?" Orville Jonas, one of the regular security guards, hurried toward me from behind the reception desk.

"Why didn't you stop her?" I slapped my key card on the panel to get outside, but the light remained red.

"Who?" Orville joined me by the door as I tried to open it.

"The woman in pink outside. The one with the weird fingers." Why wasn't my key card working?

Orville looked out into the slowly lightening dawn. "I don't see anyone. I haven't seen anyone since I started my shift seven hours ago."

I turned back to Orville. "How can you miss her? She's dressed like a fairy and lit up like a Christmas tree. Get this door open. My card is broken."

His puzzled gaze flickered over me as he pulled out his card. "Pulling an all-nighter again?"

"Yes. But this isn't the case of an overtaxed brain. She was on the top floor. I chased her. You must have seen her come in or spotted her on the cameras as she walked along the corridors."

He tried his card, but the door remained locked. "Weird. Must be a system glitch."

"So how did she get out?" I jabbed a finger at the glass.

Orville looked at me and then outside. "I don't know what to say. There's no one here but the two of us."

I turned to the glass to show him exactly where she was. She'd gone.

# Chapter 6

I'd been sitting with Orville at the reception desk for an hour, looking through the security camera footage.

"There you are again," Orville said. "You're running fast, but I can't see what or who you're running after."

My head throbbed and my stomach churned. We'd watched this footage five times and seen exactly the same thing. Me dashing around like an idiot, chasing someone who was invisible.

I pointed at the frozen image. "That's a shadow! That could be her. Run it on."

"She won't be there. We've looked through it all."

"I'm not making her up. She cast that shadow."

Orville did as I asked. No pink lady revealed herself.

He shuffled in his seat and adjusted the screen. "If you've been working all night, it's easy to see things that aren't there. I know what it's like after I've done a night shift. My brain plays tricks on me. I'm always careful when driving home, because I see things on the road that aren't there."

I glanced at him. "What kind of things?"

"It's usually shadows cast of things at the side of the road, trash cans, or lumps of earth and grass. My tired brain turns them into people or an animal about to leap in front of me. I've jabbed the brakes so many times to stop from hitting something that wasn't there." He shuffled around some more. "Maybe that's what you saw."

"I didn't imagine the woman in pink. And she saw me. She responded. She was behaving like it was a fun game." Why didn't she show up on any of the cameras?

Orville was silent as he ran through more footage.

He didn't believe me. And the more I looked into this mystery, the less surprised I was he doubted me. There wasn't a single frame with the woman on it. Could she have done something to the cameras, so they didn't detect her? Jammed the signal or interrupted the recording? There were devices that distorted a person's image, so they weren't picked up, but we had the best security system going. Gideon wasn't prepared to lose his designs or concepts to the competition.

"Wait! That was another shadow. She must have used a distortion field to get around," I said.

"What's that?"

I closed my eyes for a second and rubbed my forehead. "Something that doesn't exist. I saw it on a sci-fi show. They used resonance fields to... never mind. It was fiction." Yesterday had been a long, stressful day and a long night, and this new day wasn't getting any better.

"As soon as the new team comes in at seven, I'll tell them about this. They'll do a top-to-bottom search of the building. And I'll get them to check all the camera feeds. If she was in here, we'll find her and figure out how she got in unseen."

"That sounds like a lot of work for something I might have imagined."

"It's important. If there was a security breach, we need to plug it quickly." Orville rubbed the back of his neck. "I know you guys upstairs work on the out-there stuff. I've even had a few tries on your Enchanted Forest game. My boys love it, but it's a bit too much for me."

"What are you suggesting?" Doubt flickered through me like an unfinished spell from a wizard's wand. Combine the stress of yesterday with working too hard, not sleeping, and the worry something was wrong with me, and could this be the result? I was seeing pink ladies.

"Nothing. It's nothing. You just have active imaginations." Orville nodded at me. He had the same look in his eyes as my therapist. "We'll get to the bottom of this. Perhaps you should call it a night, though. Or a day. It's supposed to be a nice one. Take time off, get out there and see the real world. It doesn't all suck just because it's not full of witches and wizards."

"Thanks for not coming right out and saying you think I'm crazy."

He scrubbed the stubble just showing on his chin. "I've heard Mr. Masters call craziness genius or eccentricity. He told me once an insane person is just misunderstood. I asked him about all the criminals inside Forest Vale Psychiatric Hospital or the Silver Oak Asylum. He laughed and said everyone's crazy. You and me, too."

I wasn't sure how to take that comment, so I simply nodded and stood from my seat. "I need to sort some things upstairs, then I'll take a few hours off. Let me know if anything shows on the security system or you find out how that woman got inside."

"Of course. You'll get a full report. So will Mr. Masters."

I winced. Was that a good idea? If this woman was real, I'd let her escape. Maybe I'd left the door to the main office open so she could sneak in without a key card. Would Gideon think this was my fault? But if it turned out she wasn't real, I'd look like a freak. It would be another bullet in Sylvester's gun to help him take me down.

"Anything else you need?" Orville asked.

"No, thanks." I couldn't take back what I'd told him. I was certain I'd seen that woman, but I couldn't explain her floating, those weird fingers, and that strange, creepy smile. Although, if Sylvester had been drugging me, that could be the reason for my new imaginary friend.

I used the elevator to get upstairs, leaning against the closed door and keeping my eyes shut for the entire journey. There was something wrong with me. The weirdness that had been lingering in the background for months had just hit a new level of crazy. Was I heading along the path to a complete breakdown?

I finished my now cold coffee at my desk then made a call.

"Doctor Thomas's office. How may I help you?" It was Maggie.

"Morning, Maggie. This is Noah Drake. Has Tom got any sessions today?"

"Let me check his diary. He has a cancelation at four. Would that work?"

I checked my calendar and frowned. Gideon had booked in a long strategy session all afternoon. I couldn't get out of that. "Anything earlier? I could come in now."

"No, I'm sorry. If it's an emergency, we have a locum psychiatrist. She's very good."

I didn't want to talk to a stranger about breathing fire, floating above my desk, an invisible woman, and the strange red glitter that kept showing up. Tom would have a hard enough time making sense of it, let alone someone I'd had nothing to do with.

When I didn't respond, Maggie gently cleared her throat. "Perhaps a short telephone consult would be helpful? Doctor Saunders has a few minutes before his first client."

I exhaled loudly. "Please. He knows my history. I just need someone to talk to."

"Give me a few seconds. I'll get him up to speed then put you through." Soft music played down the line as Maggie put me on hold.

The line connected. "Noah! What can I do for you?"

"I'm not doing so well." I looked at the ceiling, not sure where to start. "I'm going to put everything out there and let you decide if I need to be sectioned."

"Go ahead. I'm listening." Tom's tone was neutrally professional. He'd know what to do about my crisis.

"Yesterday, I saw donuts floating. A spark of something shot out of my hand and slowed them down. I tried to do it again, but whatever it was, it wouldn't work. Then I got sick. Not puking sick, but I got a headache and my stomach churned. I went to the washroom, burped, and fire came out of my mouth. It set fire to the building, and we had to evacuate. And then I fell asleep at my desk last night. When I woke, I was floating. And this woman in pink broke into the office. She was strange looking. Her features were distorted. She had fingers that were too long... and she floated. Her feet were off the ground." I drew in a deep breath. "I don't know what's going on. Am I losing my mind? Could this be drug induced? Could any of this be real?"

"Noah, I've listened to everything you've told me. Do you feel like harming yourself or others?"

"No! Nothing like that."

"Good. How long have you been at the office?"

"I came in yesterday morning. That was when the weird stuff started happening."

"Have you been home since then?"

I pressed the bridge of my nose. "No. Things get intense during the production phase of a new game." All the phases were intense, but the creative stage got freaky.

"You fell asleep at your desk after working non-stop for how long?"

"No, it's not that. It's not the long hours making me see things."

"I know you think it isn't, but we've discussed managing your condition through reducing mental and physical overload. You believe your work is your life, and it makes you happy."

"It does."

"Stress does horrible, crazy things to the body. And an overtaxed body and a stressed mind will make you hallucinate things that aren't real."

"People floating? Sparks coming out of my hand? The fire breathing? That was all my brain having a glitch?"

"The brain is complicated and fragile. You're not sleeping, you have very little social life outside of work, and you're unhappy. You've told me this during our sessions. Could this be your brain's way of giving you a kick to make changes before something serious happens?"

"Setting fire to a building isn't serious?"

"You tell me."

I hated it when Tom answered a question with a question. "Of course. I... These things were from my imagination?"

"Did anyone else see them happen? The floating, the fire breathing, the spark coming out of your hand?"

I let out a long sigh. "No, and I've checked with security. If there was another person here, the cameras would have seen her. And she wasn't. But she was so real to me."

"If no one else saw these things, what does that suggest to you?"

My teeth ground, and I did the deep breathing exercises Tom had taught me. "It's all in my head and I'm going insane?"

"I don't think you are. But I will strongly suggest you take time off work."

"I can't take any time off."

"If you don't, you may not have a choice. Your body and mind will shut down. You won't be able to function."

"What if someone drugged me? Would that cause these hallucinations and strange feelings?"

"That's a leap."

"But not impossible?"

"There are drugs that affect the brain in such a way. Have you been experimenting?"

"No, I never touch the stuff. What if someone put something in my drink, though?"

Tom hesitated. "Then I suggest you get to a hospital and get tested. If someone is manipulating you using illegal substances, they're breaking some serious laws."

I almost slapped my forehead. Of course, it was an obvious way of finding out if Sylvester was messing with me. "How long would the drugs stay in my system?"

"It's impossible to say without knowing what you've been given. But before you fix on this idea, you must commit to looking after yourself. And consider why someone would want to drug you."

"I've never had any problems until recently. It has to be the reason."

"Six months is a long time to have feelings of paranoia."

"You don't get it. It's only recently things have escalated. And I think I know who is doing this to me. I'm not insane."

"No one said you were. One second." Tom went silent then returned. "My first client has arrived, but I'll book you in for an afternoon session and we can talk some more."

"No need. And I can't make that time. It's good. I know what I need to do. Thanks." I ended the conversation, suddenly feeling a lot better. With a blood test, I'd figure out if I was being messed with.

I set down my phone, turned, and came face-to-face with Sylvester.

# Chapter 7

Sylvester's smile had never been smugger. His gaze slowly traveled over me. "That was interesting. I always knew you were weird, just like the rest of the gaming geeks, but I didn't realize you were literally insane."

I dug my nails into my palms. "That was a private conversation. You shouldn't have crept up on me and listened."

"And you shouldn't have had a private conversation about your mental instability in a public office." He shifted his weight onto the balls of his feet. "I know you treat this place like it's your home, but for those of us who have actual lives, we know the difference."

I turned away, my cheeks hot as anger built inside me. "I need to get to work."

"No, no, no. What you need to do is convince me not to tell Gideon everything I just heard."

I froze then glanced at Sylvester as he moved to stand beside my desk, still looking disgustingly smug. "Why would you do that?"

"For fun? Because I don't like you? Because I don't feel safe working in an office with someone who is clearly troubled and potentially dangerous. Pick an option."

"We all have issues, but I'm a threat to nobody."

"The fire you set in the washroom shows otherwise." He picked up a miniature wizard figurine I'd hand painted in black and gold and turned it over. "Your false confidence may charm Gideon, but when he learns the truth, your time here will be over."

I snatched the figurine from his fingers and placed it back in its proper position on my desk. "Why do you hate me so much?"

His top lip curled. "Because you're too good to be true. You're the golden boy, and you don't deserve that role. You don't take advantage of what you have. All the options are sitting there, and you ignore them."

"Because I'm good at my job doesn't mean you get to hate me. You stick to what you're good at, and I'll do the same. We don't even have to speak to each other."

"I'm not talking about your ability to code or make up those ridiculous role-playing scenarios that get the loners and morons hot under the collar. Anyone with no social life or friends can make up loser junk like that." Sylvester gestured across the empty office. "I'm talking about all the opportunities you pass up here."

"What opportunities? I'm head of division, the games I put out land in the top ten on the chart, and I'm giving a keynote talk at the Excel Masters next year."

"Not those skills, numbskull." Sylvester shook his head. "You're so dense that it can't be an act."

"What am I supposed to be acting out?"

"All the women in Stardust Industries want you!" He yelled the words at me. "Most of the time, you act like they don't even exist. You've got them fluttering around your desk like thirsty bees after the nectar, and you're only ever nice to them. I've seen you give so many of them the brushoff. What's wrong with you? Aren't you a real man? Or do you only get hot for the fake game chicks you create?"

My eyebrows shot up. "You hate me because I don't use women?"

"You do nothing with them. You're a eunuch, while the rest of us don't get a look in because the skirts are too busy fluttering and flirting around someone who paints tiny wizards for fun." He whacked Gandalf to the floor.

I scooped him up. "Tiny wizard painting is cool. And the women who work here aren't employed to be used by anyone. Where do you get your morals, the Trump Guide to being a Douche?"

"You wouldn't know what to do with any of these skirts if you got one home. You'd probably talk about magic or show off by trying to make things float." He grated out an angry noise through his teeth. "I have no clue what they see in you. You're a scruffy mess, who doesn't even shave regularly, and you probably don't shower as often as you should. You gaming geeks are all the same."

It took a lot for me to lose my cool, but Sylvester punched my buttons. His worldview was about what he could get out of a situation. He always looked for an angle or something to manipulate. And when people behaved respectably, it highlighted him as the lowlife scumbag he was. Sylvester hated being shown up.

I turned away from him. "Get out of here. I don't have time for your egotistical bull."

"Make time. Because I know your secret, weirdo." Sylvester took a step closer then backed off when I spun around and glared at him. I wasn't a violent guy, but I could throw a punch. And I really wanted to see if I could break some bones. "Once the women in this place know you're certifiable, they won't want anything to do with you. Then I'll get my chance."

I shoved my chair out of the way. "I like the women who work here. They're incredible at their jobs. And just because I don't hit on them doesn't make me any less of a man. It's called respect."

"Your old-fashioned, pathetic values get in the way of me scoring. Even the geek with the weird colored hair turned me down. It was because of you. She was saying no to me while looking at you. You've got them all under your spell, and it makes me sick."

"I thought you didn't believe in magic."

He bared his teeth at me. "You're done here. The sooner you're gone, the better."

No, he wasn't going to win. I was a hundred times better than Sylvester, even if I was crazy. "Gideon won't fire me. I've done nothing wrong. And even if he learns I'm having a few issues, he'll understand."

"Oh, I'll make sure he understands everything. I'll tell him you threatened me."

"I didn't!"

"Everyone knows I intimidate you. And when I accidentally overheard you were about to be sent to the loony bin, you demanded I keep it under wraps, or you'd silence me."

"Which would prove you're a sneak and can't be trusted."

His face flushed a dull red. "Maybe I received a call from your concerned therapist, who thought you were a threat. Gideon won't allow an unstable lunatic to work for him, no matter how much money you make him."

"Don't be so sure about that. Gideon is all about taking risks. Maybe he'll bet on crazy."

"And then, of course, there are the rumors of you leaking company secrets to the competition."

I lunged at him, and he dodged out of the way. "Liar! Keep your mouth shut. I'd never do that."

Sylvester backed away, but he was smiling as he realized he'd shoved me over the edge. "You didn't mean to, but someone approached you when you were in a bar, and you thought he was a wizard. He promised to tell you the secrets of magic and how to find your way into the worlds you dream up in exchange for information about Stardust Industries. How could you resist? You told him everything, then he knocked you out with a spell and left."

"I'll knock you out," I growled. "You make everyone's life here less enjoyable. You're the one who should be fired."

He shrugged. "Of course, all this could go away. I could forget we ever had this conversation."

"Why would you do that? You never do anything other than help yourself."

His head wobbled from side to side and a humorless smile appeared. "If you agree to give me eighty percent of the profit you make from the Haven Witch game when it releases, I'll have sudden memory loss." Sylvester's smile grew shark-like. "Do we have a deal?"

"Get lost. I deserve the bonus coming from that game. I've been working with the team on it for almost a year."

"As have I. Yet Gideon doesn't include profit shares from the games in my package. He says I'm more of an admin guy." Sylvester huffed out a laugh. "I'm not here to do the filing or paperwork."

"Why not? It suits you, clearing up after other people. You should wrap an apron around your middle and start serving the drinks."

Sylvester slammed a hand on my desk. "Take the deal, or I'll speak to Gideon and then let all the ladies in Stardust Industries know you're cuckoo."

My hands flexed, but I tried to appear nonchalant, even though I was sweating. "Do it. Let's see who he believes."

Sylvester's expression soured, and he looked down his nose at me. "Don't test me. I've ruined other people's careers. I can do the same to you."

"If I'm forced out, I'll take my knowledge and work for someone else. Or I'll set up my own business."

"Not for two years, you won't. Don't forget the non-compete clause in your contract. The only work you'll be good for is dishwashing in the back of a restaurant. That's if you're not locked up in the loony bin."

My gut churned, and another headache grew. Sylvester was spiteful enough to go through with this threat. And although Gideon had my back, if the rumors got too loud about my mental instability, he might sideline me, put me on gardening leave, or straight out fire me to avoid a scandal.

"What will you have if you don't have this place?" Sylvester said softly. "What's waiting for you at home? A loving wife, kids, the pet dog? Who will you lean on when the going gets tough?"

He'd just hit my weak spot. "I have other things going on. Friends, people who care about me."

"Sure. Is there anyone you don't pay who cares about you?" Sylvester said. "I'm assuming you were talking to some over-priced therapist. He wouldn't care if you were dead or alive if you weren't paying him by the hour."

I scrubbed my fingers through my hair. "You can't take eighty percent. I've got plans for that money."

"So have I. And you don't need it. You're barely at home, and you wear the same clothes every day. Any money you spend goes on takeout coffee or geek gaming gear. I can't remember the last time you took a vacation."

"I take vacations." I scrubbed my forehead as the ache behind my eyes grew.

"Not for at least three years. I feel sorry for you."

"I feel so much better knowing that." I lowered my hand. "That's my money."

"You don't deserve it. And you can't spend it in la-la land. It's better if I take it from you."

"You mean if you steal it by spreading lies about me?"

Sylvester shrugged. "Your only network of support will be gone if I decide to make it happen. Don't think Jed, Tony, and the other geeks will bother with you once you're a nobody out on the street. They'll forget you once the new golden boy arrives. And this time, I'll have a say in the recruitment. We don't need another goodie two shoes sliding in and ruining things." He turned as the office door opened and Gideon walked in. "Time's up. You get to decide your future right now. Gideon, over here."

"Don't you dare," I hissed out.

"I love a dare," Sylvester said. "Want to see how dark I'm prepared to go?"

That scum sucking, lowlife, dirt bag. He'd ruin my life out of spite. My pulse raced as Gideon approached, an easy swagger in his step, his dark suit immaculate, and his hair swept off his face.

"You're both in early," he said. "Something exciting happening with the game?"

"We were just talking about Haven Witch," Sylvester said. "And I was making a bet with Noah."

"I enjoy a wager," Gideon said. "Let me in on the action. What's at stake?"

"This is an informal thing between the two of us." Sylvester patted me hard on the back. "Noah was deciding if he was man enough to take the risk."

"Sylvester, don't go too hard on him. Noah needs his head in Haven Witch, not worrying if he'll lose a fistful of cash to you." Gideon tsked, but appeared amused by the situation.

"With the bonus he's about to get when Haven Witch is a smash, he won't worry about losing a little money?" Sylvester turned a feral smile to me. "Are you in or out?"

I gulped down my panic. I couldn't lose this job. Even if Gideon took my side and supported me over my failing sanity, it might only be in the short term while I finish Haven Witch. After that, he would dump me because I was too much of a risk.

And what if I couldn't get my head fixed? What if Tom signed me off and said I wasn't fit for work? I couldn't lose what I had. Sylvester knew me better than I realized. I had so little outside of this office. I lived and breathed games. It was the only thing I was passionate about.

Gideon chuckled. "It looks like you've gotten him over a barrel. You need to decide. Don't let Sylvester get one over on you. He can be sly like that."

"Noah doesn't mind. He knows life is all one big game. It's what he lives for. The crazy world of magic." Sylvester smirked.

If I lost that money to Sylvester, it wouldn't be the end of the world. My plans would have to shift back, but I could still achieve what I wanted. None of that would be possible if I lost my reputation.

"The clock is ticking, and we're all busy people." Gideon glanced over his shoulder.

"Last chance," Sylvester said. "How crazy are you, Noah?"

"I'm in. I accept the deal."

Gideon spread his hands out and clapped them together. "Excellent. It's good to see my team working so well together while having fun. It makes the job worthwhile."

"I couldn't agree more," Sylvester said. "Right decision, Noah. We can deal with the formalities later."

"But no more distractions," Gideon said. "We present Haven Witch to the board in two weeks. You need to be ready."

"We're on schedule." I glowered at Sylvester. "Nothing will get in the way of making this succeed."

Gideon leaned forward and brushed my left shoulder. "More red glitter! Tell your girlfriend to ease off of this stuff. She may think it's cute, but it's tacky." He walked away with Sylvester while I stared at the sheen of red glitter on my shoulder and sighed.

What had I gotten myself into?

⌘

I blinked my gritty eyes and spent a few seconds stretching my arms over my head.

"I feel you, buddy." Jed sat opposite me. "I wouldn't mind laying on a rack and having my kinks pulled out straight. All this hunching is killer on the spine."

"Game design is not for the weak," I said.

Jed nodded, his dark gaze serious for once. "Is everything good with you? You've barely said a word all day."

"I'm just focused. Been tangling with this coding issue for hours." And stewing over how to kill Sylvester and get away with it.

"Coding glitches don't usually make you this quiet. And you missed out on the cookie run. Tegan got a deluxe box of fancy caramel things with frosting. I don't think you even heard me when I said they were in the kitchen."

"I'm not in the mood for cookies."

"Okay." Jed twisted in his seat. "You're sure there's nothing wrong, though? Other than the coding?"

"It's work stress. And Sylvester was a jerk earlier today."

Jed clicked his fingers. "Of course. Don't think about that idiot. He'll be picking on someone else tomorrow." He grabbed his backpack and parka off the back of his seat. "I'd stay and help you with the coding, but I've got a hot date with a dungeon mistress."

"Sounds like fun."

"Best fun I've had in weeks. She's amazing." He paused by my desk. "You should find yourself a dungeon mistress. She'd take your mind off Sylvester's sneaky tactics."

"I'll get signed up to Dungeon Mistress Dating, shall I?"

Jed clapped me on the shoulder. "It's worth a shot. Hey, you've got a private message."

I glanced at the right-hand corner of my screen to see my inbox flashing. Few people had access to my personal account, and anyone who used it knew not to send pictures of dancing cats while I worked.

"Maybe some hot mistress of the dungeon wants to play with you, too. Have a fun night." Jed headed away from my desk and out the door.

I hovered my mouse over the message and clicked it.

*Got time for a lonely witch, looking to defeat the bad guys?*

# Chapter 8

I was so glad I'd said yes to the enigmatic message I'd received in my inbox. After the day I'd had, I'd needed some light relief and a way to forget my troubles. What I got was something so much better.

I'd found a gaming unicorn. And after playing with Witch Turner for most of the night, I was already a little in love with her.

"Watch your right side. Goblins at your three o'clock." Witch Turner's melodic voice came through my earphones as we played the Empire of Vampires game.

"On it. Using a thunderbolt."

"Be careful of ricochet. That spell can misbehave."

I angled my shot and destroyed half a dozen goblins.

"Ten out of ten. Are you sure you didn't design this game?" Witch Turner laughed. "You know all the secrets."

I sent her a smiley face over the game messaging system. "No, but I know the guy who did. He never shares his cheats."

"That means you're naturally brilliant at all games. I kind of hate you."

"Only some of them. Well, most of them."

She laughed again. "We need a rest break. My energy is down to thirty percent. And I need food. In real life, too. I haven't eaten for six hours."

"I can share some with you. I have rations in my pack." Or rather, my avatar, Fire Fang, had rations.

"Yum! Hellhound rations. It had better not be raw meat. Let's head to those caves and recharge. I've got a potion I can swap for food."

"It's a deal."

"You don't even want to know what it is? I could offer you a stink bomb potion."

"I trust you. You haven't killed me yet."

"The night is still young, my furry friend. Follow me."

My avatar, Fire Fang, followed the striking, dark-haired six-foot witch along a stony pathway and into a small series of caves. After she'd checked them out, she picked one, and we went inside.

The Empire of Vampires game was true to life, meaning you needed regular rest periods; otherwise, your character died of exhaustion. This was the perfect time to get to know Witch Turner better. I'd already figured out she was funny as all hell and an incredible gamer, but there was more I needed to know.

We did our trade, my food for her potion, which turned out to be a handy invisibility potion, and settled in, our avatars building a small fire and then resting beside it.

"I'm glad you're on my side. I'd be toast by now if you were the enemy," I said. "And I've never gotten this far in the game before."

"Always glad to be of service to a novice gamer."

"Novice! You think I'm new to this?"

"You said you weren't good at all games."

"I was being modest."

"And doing a terrible job." Crunching hit my ears. "Sorry, just stuffing in the chips."

"Go for it."

"This game is one of my favorites, although there's not enough magic. A world is never perfect unless it's full of magic and mystery."

I sighed. "I wish it was real in our world."

"You don't think it is?"

I opened my mouth to make a joke, but I didn't want to. After all the weirdness I'd been through, there was a small part of me that believed magic was behind it. We didn't know everything about this world. We had theories about how things operated, but the best scientists worked to disprove their own theories and results. It was possible that one day magic would be proven to be real.

"Hey, are you still there? I've not grossed you out by munching cheesy crunch triangles, have I?" Witch Turner said.

"Nope. I'm just thinking. I didn't want to scare you off by saying something dumb."

"Did you miss me killing those six vampires? It takes a lot to scare me."

"That was impossible to miss. I got covered in gore."

"Because you stood too close, trying to defend my honor. It's an honor I can look after. Although it's nice to have a handsome fanged killer with fur standing beside me."

"You think I'm handsome?"

"I think your avatar of a hulking hybrid wolf who can snap the enemy in half is handsome."

My mouth twisted to the side. "You like the alpha guys in real life?"

"I like someone who is kind and brave in their own way. Not someone who goes out and slays dragons to prove themselves or puts other people down to make themselves look good," Witch Turner said. "People who have a purpose and a vision for how they want their life to be. Those who drift or make do with things because they've always been a certain way miss out on so much."

I let out a quiet sigh of relief. "I know what you mean. It took me a while to follow my gaming passion. My parents died when I was barely out of my teens, but they always told me I'd never make a living designing games. I tried to stamp on my dream, but it burned in the background. Even after I'd done a degree in economics, it's all I wanted to do."

"I'm sorry you lost your parents, but they were wrong to prevent you from following your dream. I'm glad you had the courage to make it happen," Witch Turner said.

"I'm not sure about courage. It was more of an obsession. I had to get the imaginary worlds and people out of my head before I went crazy. They wouldn't stop talking to me."

Witch Turner giggled, and the sound tickled at the base of my spine. The feeling unfolded into a welcome warmth I hadn't felt for a long time. "I'm the same. I dream about the games I play. I imagine casting spells and smiting the bad guys in real life, too. There's nothing I'd like more than making sure the world gets all the magic it deserves."

"What about you? Are you following your dreams? If you tell me you're a game designer too, I think I might lose my heart forever."

"That's sweet of you to say. No, I don't design games. This is a hobby. I don't have your talent or experience."

"What do you do, then?"

She paused for several seconds. "I run a candy store. It's a new thing. I'm testing out a few pop-up stores in different places. I want to see if I can be-spell people with my magical candy. I want to make them so obsessed with my treats that they come to the store every day, demanding more and wanting to try everything I've created."

"A candy making witch. That sounds fun. You must have a sweet tooth."

"I love treats. How about you? Do you have a favorite candy you can never resist?"

"So long as it's not donuts, I don't mind. I'll try anything."

"What's wrong with donuts?"

"Oh, I had a bad experience not so long ago." Witch Turner was growing on me, but I wasn't ready to reveal all my quirks. "How long have you been running a candy store?"

"Not long. I tried lots of things before this. I enjoy doing things that allow me to travel and explore new places and meet people. I love meeting people with potential and watching them grow."

"You mentor them?"

"Um... kind of. It's more like I let them see the options available to them. It's nothing formal or educational. I just like getting people to explore a different way of living. One not confined by traditional beliefs and values. I'm not sure if I'm making much sense."

"It sounds incredible. I've always wanted to mentor young gamers. It's tough to break into this industry. It takes more than an obsession with the games. You have to have a passion for what goes on behind the scenes, learn the foundations of what makes a winning game." I'd always wanted a mentor when I was a kid, but had fought alone to get my place. "In the future, I'm opening my own business, and it'll have a charitable foundation to support future gamers from disadvantaged backgrounds. Just like you, I want to show them there's another world out there."

"One full of magic and surprises?"

"Exactly! And it'll be away from the inner cities and the hustle of the commercial districts. Game design can be done anywhere in the world. I want a place in the country with a separate annex for the mentees. It'll be an all-inclusive way of living, where they learn the elements of game design, but also experience a different life. They'll be encouraged to follow a dream most give up on because others tell them it's not possible."

"Sounds idyllic. You have such a huge heart. It'll be a massive success," Witch Turner said. "When are you setting this up?"

I scowled at the screen. "I was thinking in the next three years, but my plans just took a hit. It may not be for another ten years."

"Why? I know you can't say much about your work, but I can tell you're someone high up in the gaming world. You must earn a fortune."

"And you know that how?"

"Would you believe me if I said I cast a spell?"

"Almost. You still haven't told me how you got my personal email." I'd asked her several times, but Witch Turner had been evasive about how she'd found me and what she knew about me.

"I may not be a gaming genius, but I know systems, and I'm an ace at researching. I also figured you'd be fun to play with. Someone with a similar skill set to me. And I was right."

"You're saying you hacked the email server I use?"

"Shush! I'm saying nothing. Walls have ears if you get your privacy settings wrong."

"How did you do it?"

"My lips are sealed." She crunched more chips. "If it's any comfort, I'm only interested in having wolfy fun, not your big bucks."

I was stunned Witch Turner had accessed the server. She'd have needed to get through the permissions and privileges, firewall, backups, and ensure the server log didn't send an alert.

But I didn't mind Witch Turner pursuing me. It was a tremendous compliment to have someone so skilled in gaming interested in forming a team.

"So... still want to play with a hacker? If you're worried about the file of dirty pictures I found on your hard drive, I won't tell anyone." There was a teasing note in her voice.

"Funny! Of course, yes. We have to get to the next level. And to answer your question about my plans, I do make great money. The latest game I'm working on shows promise. If the early beta testing is anything to go by, it'll be a hit."

"What's it called?"

"State secret."

"Hmmm, did you have anything to do with the Avalon game?"

I tensed in my seat. "Err... maybe. Do you like it?"

"I love it. I'm excited to see what you do next. And I saw Stardust Industries release something about an upcoming game called Haven Witch. Is that you? Please say it is."

Doubt flickered through me. I couldn't share too much. Gamers were sneaky, and it wasn't unheard of for them to make false friendships to get sensitive information from game designers.

When I didn't reply, she laughed. "It's okay. I promise I won't steal your secrets and sell them to anyone. And I understand if you can't tell me. I'm sure, whatever you're working on, it'll be amazing. I'll still beat you, though, even if you have all the cheat codes."

"I'm glad you understand. I love to talk about the games, but..."

"Say no more. Your boss will destroy you if you pillow talk."

"Pillow talk!"

"You think this is a honey trap, right? My hot witch avatar is wearing down your defenses."

"I... well, maybe. It happens."

"It's not. We won't talk about what you're working on anymore. We'll just play together. Deal?"

I didn't want to stop talking to Witch Turner. There was a connection here, and I wasn't ready to let it go. "The game I'm working on isn't the problem." I leaned back in my chair and looked at the ceiling. "I work with someone who's making my life difficult. He's got something on me, and to keep him quiet, it means giving him money."

Her gasp shot through my earphones. "Someone is blackmailing you?"

"Yeah. He overheard me talking to someone and filled in the gaps about what I've been hiding."

"You didn't kill someone, did you?"

"No! Well, only in these games."

"Hurt someone?"

"No one got hurt."

"Theft, arson, assault?"

"No to all of those things."

"Well, it can't be that bad, then. I just needed to check I wasn't hitting on a psychopath."

"You're hitting on me?"

"Oh, boy. You totally missed the important part of that sentence."

I grinned and rubbed the back of my neck. "I'm not dangerous. But reputation is everything in this business. This guy will keep my secret, so long as I share some of my profits from an upcoming game release."

"Fire Fang! That's terrible. What kind of scummy individual does that? You work with him?"

"I do. Everyone knows him as The Sneak. He loves listening in on private conversations and getting the dirt on people. The trouble is, he's my boss's right-hand man. If I rock the boat too much, I'll be the one that gets thrown out."

"If you're as amazing at designing games as you are at playing them, this sneaky jerk would never convince the boss to let you go."

"This industry is weirdly insular. Everyone knows each other's business, even though we all try to keep it a secret. Even if he decided not to speak to the boss, he could leak information about me into the public domain." My scowl returned as I dwelled on Sylvester's treachery. "When it comes time for me to leave or set up my own business, I won't get anywhere. I couldn't get financial backing or support. No one would want to know me."

"You can set up, anyway. You'll have your country house with your baby gamers in a beautiful village. And I expect you'll fill the house with children, animals, and a brilliant wife." Witch Turner paused. "I suppose you've got one of those?"

I grinned. "Actually, no. It's hard to find a sympathetic wife who knows the games will always come before her."

"You've been hanging out with the wrong ladies. There must be women working in the gaming industry. You should go out with them."

"Maybe. It's complicated. There's someone I like, but she's out of my reach."

"If you have someone, there's no chance, then?"

"No chance for what?"

"The two of us to go on epic adventures together in real life."

I sat forward in my seat. My spine stiffened, and my hands clenched. Here was a real woman I connected with. She hadn't come from my imagination. She was on the other side of this game. If I wanted to, I could meet her. We had a genuine connection. Her humor was sharp and clever. She asked so many questions my head spun, and she knew her games. Why was I hesitating?

"Um... did I say too much? Sorry, I can get intense, but it's rare I find anyone I like who's into the same things as me. When you were describing your dream, you were basically saying what I want, too. I'd love to have a house in a beautiful place and to fill it with creative, kind people. Of course, I want a vast room where I can play games for hours with no one else around, but I long to share that with someone. Maybe even someone like you."

"I... I'm kind of stunned to hear that."

"Sorry, there I go again, getting all weirdly obsessive when we've only been playing for one night. I should let you go. I'm tired, and I'm saying stupid things. And if I only eat processed junk and not some real food soon, I'll get jittery. Too many E numbers."

I couldn't let this chance get away. "You aren't saying anything stupid. I know where you're coming from. I work with people in the gaming industry all the time, but this is different. I feel it, too. I like you, Witch Turner. I love gaming with you. We should meet, see if we get on as well in the real world."

"I don't know. You think the only thing we'll have in common is slaying vampires and destroying goblins?" There was a vulnerability I hadn't heard in her voice until now. It made me like her even more.

I drew in a deep breath. "There's only one way to find out."

"We have to deal with your work issue first, though. Make sure your dream is kept on track."

"What do you mean?"

"Your office jerk. He's holding you back. You should go for it. What you want to do is nothing short of miraculous." She giggled again. "And I know exactly what we should do to him."

"What's that?"

"Add him to a game and destroy him." Witch Turner burst into laughter.

I chuckled along with her. "I'll write the code for that later. We can have exclusive access and pound him into the ground."

"Sounds great. We'll destroy him the next time we do battle."

I stifled a yawn behind my hand as a wave of exhaustion hit. We'd been playing for six hours.

"Hey, Fire Fang, you're tired. So am I. And you need some rest. I expect you're working tomorrow," Witch Turner said.

"Yeah, I work every day, especially in the middle of a new game design. But... I really would like to meet you."

A soft sigh hit my ears and made my heart clench.

"Soon. I promise, we'll meet really soon. Good night, Fire Fang."

# Chapter 9

Five hours of blissful sleep later and I strolled into the office, feeling like my feet barely touched the plush carpeted floor.

"There you are," Tony said. "We figured you'd run away with the goblins."

"You're not sick, are you?" Jed held up two fingers in the sign of the cross.

"I'm fine. Just caught up on some long overdue sleep. You should try it sometime." I dropped my backpack and slid off my jacket. The night I'd spent gaming with Witch Turner had been the best. When I'd gotten home, I'd crashed and slept solidly, dreaming about actually meeting her.

"You look... different," Tony said.

"How?" I scraped a hand through my hair.

"Healthy. You're worrying us," Jed said. "You're not on those juice shots again, are you? Those things make you go blind. Too many anti-oxidants."

"Relax. Everything is great. I'll figure out that coding glitch today, and then we can work on the side characters. Get your plans together so we can go over them." The instant I turned on my computer, I spotted a flashing message in my inbox.

Excitement swirled inside me as I opened it and found it was from Witch Turner.

*Had an amazing night. Looking forward to a rematch.*

I grinned as I replied. *Me, too. Are you free tonight?*

*Always for you. And I've got new spells to try. They'll blow your socks off.*

"Who are you talking to?"

I jumped as Jed's voice came from behind me. He was peering at my screen.

"A new friend."

His eyes gleamed. "A female friend?"

I shut down the message. "Yeah. She's cool. She's an amazing gamer."

"What specialty?" Tony said.

"Advanced spell casting. And she's got a wicked blade she's not afraid to use. We spent hours fighting the goblin king. Got to level fourteen."

"I've been trying to break through to that level for months. I helped design the damn thing, and I still can't get to the end." Jed thumped me on the arm. "You need to give me the secret back door codes."

"No codes. We didn't cheat. We got through because of Witch Turner's amazing gaming skills."

"Nice name. Is her avatar cute?" Tony said.

"Full on witch. Pale skin and jet black hair. She wears a lot of black, too."

"Uh-oh, look out. Sylvester the Sneak is coming to rain despair on us all." Jed hurried back to his chair and hunched over his keyboard.

I focused on my screen as I fired up the coding matrix.

Unsurprisingly, Sylvester stopped by my desk. "You're late."

"Technically, I'm on time. My official working hours don't begin till eight in the morning." I kept looking at the screen. If I didn't make eye contact, he wasn't real.

"You're never in this late. What's going on? Not getting second thoughts about our... arrangement?"

"Nothing's changed." Although it felt like everything had. I no longer cared about Sylvester's bullying tactics. I just wanted to get back to Witch Turner. She made me feel comfortable and normal. I was still surprised I'd revealed so much about what I wanted in my future, but she'd been easy to chat to. It felt like I'd known her all my life.

"Don't get any clever ideas." Sylvester leaned down so only I could hear him.

I glanced at him. "Don't worry, you'll get what you deserve."

His eyes narrowed, and he stepped away. "Get to work, all of you. Gideon's not happy with how long this is taking." He turned and stomped away, angry he hadn't been able to rile me. But nothing could sour my great mood. And it was all thanks to Witch Turner.

"I see Sylvester's still gunning for you," Jed said. "You must have done something bad to wind him up."

"He doesn't like my face," I said.

"You're not worried he'll snitch on you to Gideon about some made up bull?" Tony said. "I heard he did underhanded things in the last place he worked to get his own way. Several people resigned or were fired because of him."

"I'm good. And Haven Witch will be incredible. That's what we focus on."

"So that's the name of the new game?" Jed said. "I heard it going around. It's a definite?"

"I'm almost certain. I may switch things around, but no big changes. We'll go with that for now."

"Then let's get to work on making Haven Witch incredible," Tony said.

I spent the rest of the morning working with the guys and ironing out snagging issues with the supporting characters in Haven Witch.

I felt great and wasn't having odd symptoms or paranoia. Everything was back to normal. Stress caused the floating, fire breathing, and that invisible woman I'd chased around the building.

My therapist was right. I needed more sleep, less caffeine, a better social life, and to worry less. Life was for living in the real world. Well, with a healthy dose of online gaming with my favorite new gamer.

"Noah, a word." Gideon strode over.

"Everything okay?"

"Nothing too concerning, but the board meeting has been moved forward a week. Our overseers are eager to get the first iteration of Haven Witch. You need to be ready with a full presentation for them."

Sylvester hurried over, looking harassed. He handed Gideon a mug and then glared at me. The poor guy hated to be left out.

"That's fine. We're on top of things. I'll have something to wow the board with," I said.

"You'll need to put in longer hours to make it happen," Sylvester said. "No slacking off like you did this morning."

Gideon's eyebrows rose. "I've never seen Noah slack off. He's always one of the first here and one of the last to leave."

"Not today. He came in at eight." Sylvester smirked at me.

Gideon turned and looked down at Sylvester. "And that's a problem? Is Noah getting behind on Haven Witch?"

Sylvester blinked. "No, well, he could be. I'm suspicious of what these gamers do. They're always messing around."

"Noah and his team do incredible work." There was an icy edge to Gideon's voice. "I have no doubts he'll provide a first rate performance at the board meeting."

Sylvester stood there, mute with rage, his plugged hairline turning pink.

"Don't you have travel plans to arrange?" Gideon said. "And don't put me in that hotel I was in the last time. It was only four-stars."

"Of course. I'm working on your travel arrangements." Sylvester looked far less smug and a lot more peeved than he had a minute ago. "I wanted to make sure the plans for Haven Witch weren't going wrong, though. I've heard worrying rumors about this team."

"Noah said it's not a problem. I trust him. Do you have any reason not to?"

"No! Well, I'm just making sure everything runs smoothly, so you have nothing to worry about."

"It is running smoothly," I said. "The team has no issues."

"But with Noah coming in late today, I was concerned he was losing interest in the project." Sylvester tugged at his collar. "Haven Witch is important to you. He can't mess this up because he gets distracted."

"It's important to all of us," Gideon said. "And as the prime creator of Haven Witch, Noah will do everything he has to, to ensure the presentation and launch go without a hitch. I have every faith in him."

It was my turn to look smug. "I appreciate that, Gideon. There are no problems. Sylvester is worrying about nothing."

Sylvester looked like he was biting his tongue, longing to reveal my secret. If he did, he'd lose out on a chunk of money. I was interested to see which way he'd go. Was his malevolent streak enough that he'd call me out, or would his greed win over and he'd keep biting his tongue?

"I'll finalize your travel plans." Sylvester skulked away and slammed the main door behind him.

Jed and Tony looked at me and grinned. It felt good to get one over on Sylvester. Even though he was taking me to the cleaners so Gideon wouldn't find out about my issues, I still felt like I'd just won a battle.

"I won't hold you up," Gideon said. "I'll get Sylvester to send the new details of the board meeting."

After Gideon left, we settled in for another session of coding. I'd been working on a tricky issue with a graphics program for an hour when the hairs on the back of my neck stood up.

I looked up from my computer, expecting to see someone looking at me. Everyone else had their heads down.

I shook off the feeling and focused on the screen, but it returned twice as strong a few moments later. I turned my seat around so I had a full view of the office. There was no one in the corridor looking in at me, but that itchy, tense feeling when you know someone is watching you hammered through my head.

"I'm taking a five-minute break. Anyone want coffee?" I said.

Neither Jed nor Tony acknowledged me. They were like me when they got immersed in a complex game situation. Nothing else mattered.

I grabbed my empty mug and headed to the kitchenette. I cleared my throat several times to dislodge a tickle, but it only grew worse. I coughed, and it sounded more like a growl. I'd better not be getting sick. Being ill was unproductive when on such a tight schedule.

As I waited for the kettle to boil, an intense smell of honey filled my nose. I inhaled deeply, looking around the kitchen, expecting to find a pile of cakes. There was nothing. I checked in both fridges. No cakes, but the smell still lingered.

I made my coffee and left it on the counter. Every time I inhaled, I got a nose full of that smell. Although it was initially sweet, there was a strange tang to it, almost like the scent of rot. It turned my stomach, but I couldn't leave it alone.

I headed back into the main office, inhaling deeply, still coughing, sounding more like a wolf than a person.

My nose led me to the back of the office where the finance team worked. The area was almost empty. There were a couple of people working, but everyone else must have been on lunch break.

I sniffed again. The scent of honey was intense, and it was coming from the finance director's office. Janis Jolin had an impressive glass walled corner office to herself. I knew little about her, but she'd always been polite and professional when we'd spoken.

After checking no one was watching, I tried her door. It opened. The second I stepped inside, the honey smell was so intense it made my nose tingle.

I stood at the entrance and looked around. Could it be a problem with the ventilation system? There was something stuck in the vents that was wafting this weird smell around? I had a quick look around the office, not touching anything on Janis's desk, but couldn't locate the source.

When I got to her chair, I stopped and inhaled. It smelled like it was coming from under her desk. Had she gotten food under there she'd forgotten about and it had gone off? If that was the case, wouldn't she be able to smell it, too?

I eased back her chair and ducked under the foot well. No dodgy looking brown paper bags full of forgotten lunch oozing in a dark corner.

Footsteps approached the office, and I froze as the door was pushed open.

"I'm back in the office. I'll send you those figures in an hour. Yes, look over them and get back to me if you have any concerns." It was Janis.

I didn't know what to do. There was no way I could explain why I was hiding under her desk.

Janis paced across her office to the window. "Hi, Hayley. I'm still waiting for last month's report from your department. I need to tally the numbers. I know you're a couple of people down, but the board meeting has been pushed forward, and they'll expect a full account of the figures. Can you get them to me by first thing tomorrow morning? Excellent. Don't make me chase you." She paced around for a few more seconds.

While she'd been talking, I'd shuffled back as far as I could into the foot well, but it was a tight squeeze. I silently wished for her to leave. All I needed was ten seconds to get out of there.

But my wish wasn't granted. Janis walked around the desk and pulled back her chair.

I held my breath and closed my eyes. If only I could invoke a spell of invisibility.

She took a second to start up her computer, arranged a few things on her desk, and then sat in her seat and shuffled forward. Her knees hit me a few seconds later, and she froze.

Janis jerked the chair back, and she leaped up. Her startled face appeared. "Noah Drake!"

"Err... hey, Janis. I... how are you?"

She blinked several times.

When Janis didn't speak, I shuffled forward. "I expect finding me here is a surprise."

She snapped her jaw shut, and her gaze traveled over me several times. "I should say this is a surprise. Have you been waiting under there long?"

I cringed. "Not long. And I have an explanation."

She arched a groomed eyebrow, and a sly smile crossed her face. "You naughty man."

"Excuse me?"

"I've often wondered about you. I had no idea you liked older women. But it makes sense, since I've heard the talk about you turning down every date anyone's asked you on. Now, I know why."

"No! I'm not hitting on you."

"You're hiding under my desk because you wanted to give me a foot rub?" Janis chuckled and smoothed her hands over her skirt. "Why don't you come out and we can talk?"

"I'm sorry about any misunderstanding. It's just there was a weird smell in the building. It led me here." I shuffled out on my butt and stood.

"A smell under my desk? You didn't think to report it to maintenance?"

"I... no. I'm not sure why I didn't do that." I rubbed my forehead. My nose had taken over, and I hadn't been thinking straight. All I'd been focused on was that smell.

"There's no need to be coy. You thought you'd hide under my desk until I came back from lunch." Her sly smile grew, as did my panic. "Then we could have some discreet fun."

"No! It looks bad me being here, but I promise I'm not looking for fun."

Janis waved away my comment. "I know what you want."

"I should get going."

"I wish you'd told me you were coming, even though I appreciate the surprise. I could have pushed back my afternoon meetings. Still, we've got five minutes." Janis strode over, flicked the blinds closed, and shut the door.

"Janis, you're a great lady, and I really respect you. I'd never lurk under your desk with plans to... err... seduce you." Oh man, how could I get out of this without offending her?

She sashayed over and pressed a finger to my lips then slid her other hand up and down my arm. "You don't have to be shy. I know what you want, and I'm more than willing to give it to you." Janis threw herself into my arms. Her mouth slammed against mine, and I staggered back, hitting the desk.

I gripped the tops of her arms and tried to pull her off me, but she was attached like a barnacle on a sunken ship. I squirmed beneath her, twisting my face away to stop the unwanted kiss.

"Relax. No one will come in. Stop worrying. Let's have fun," she breathed into my mouth.

The office door slammed open. "Hey! Is this lady bothering you?"

I looked over and a thunderbolt of shock hit me. Winter stood in the doorway.

# Chapter 10

I was so shocked by seeing my dream woman that I stopped fighting Janis and her roving hands. "Winter?"

The tall, slender, pale-skinned brunette tilted her head and gave me a strange look. "If you don't want that woman pawing you, tell her to stop. Assault goes both ways. Of course, if you're happy for this to continue, I'll leave."

Janis spluttered an unintelligible word and slid off me, straightening her skirt and smoothing her hair. "I can assure you, whoever you are, Noah is a willing participant. I'm not assaulting him. He was waiting for me."

I struggled off the desk, staring at Winter, too afraid to blink in case she disappeared. "How are you here?"

She marched into the office, glaring at Janis. "I came to see you. I didn't expect to find you in the arms of another woman."

"I wasn't." Well, I was technically being pinned to the desk by another woman, but that wasn't the point. "I... I don't know what's going on. You're real? Janis, you see her, too?"

"Of course I see her! Do you have permission to be here?" Janis's face was flushed and her lipstick smudged. "You're not my two o'clock appointment."

"I have permission. And I came to see him." Winter nodded at me.

"You know this woman?" Janis's scowl shifted from Winter to me.

I stared at Winter again, and she gave a tiny nod and widened her eyes. "Sure. I know her. Her name is Winter."

Her mouth turned up at one corner. "That's his nickname for me. We have cute couple nicknames for each other. Although we won't be a couple for much longer if he was a willing participant in this molestation. We're exclusive."

"Molestation! Noah, I had no idea you were in a relationship." Janis turned her glare on me. "Why were you under my desk if you had no interest in seducing me?"

I pointed at the desk. "The weird honey smell. I told you. Although it's not so strong anymore."

"That's a ridiculous excuse. You've embarrassed yourself and me. And your girlfriend is clearly unhappy with you. I don't blame her. Winter, this is all his fault! Noah said nothing about you. He came after me!"

"Too right I'm angry. I show up to surprise my guy, and you're plastered all over him. I should have a word with your human resources department and see what they think about a woman in your position taking advantage of a young guy like Noah." Winter cocked one hip and rested a hand on it. "You're the senior staff member. I hope you're not taking advantage of your position, Janis."

Janis fiddled with her gold chain then sighed. "Perhaps I overstepped. Noah, if I misinterpreted your interest, then that is regretful. I didn't mean to make you uncomfortable. I really thought... well, that doesn't matter. Don't come into my office again without an appointment. We don't need any more crossed wires occurring."

"Absolutely. I agree. I should have been clearer about why I was here," I said.

"You don't want me to report what I saw to human resources, Noah?" Winter laid heavy emphasis on my name.

"No, it's good. And sorry you had to see that. I guess I have some making up to do?"

Winter gave a dramatic sigh. "You're so gorgeous, I'm surprised I'm not prying women off you every day." She stepped into Janis's personal space. "A friendly word of warning. Stay away from my guy. He's not available to anyone but me. Got it?"

"Loud and clear." Janis took a step back. "I'd appreciate it if you'd both leave."

Winter knocked the tip of her black boots against Janis's designer red heels. "Don't you need to say something first?"

Her eyebrows shot up. "Like what?"

"How about a sincere apology to both of us for potentially destroying our relationship? And an assurance you won't be molesting any other unfortunate men again. Abusing your position of power is shameful."

"I never... fine. Noah, I'm sorry. And Winter, is that your name?"

Winter shrugged and nodded. "It'll do."

"Well, Winter, I'm sorry we met under these circumstances. Of course, if I'd known Noah was in a relationship, I'd have never gone near him."

"Thanks. And Janis, I'm sorry, too," I said.

She accepted my fumbled apology with more grace than I deserved.

I glanced at Winter. I was in shock over her super possessive statement about me being her guy. She wasn't even real, so how could she lay claim? But this wasn't a delusion, since Janis could see her, too.

It was clear Janis felt unsettled because she scuttled behind her desk, using it as a shield against Winter's intimidation tactics.

"Let's go, honey." Winter held her hand out to me, and after a second of hesitation, I grabbed it, and we left the office.

She giggled as she looked at me, still holding my hand. "That was fun. But why do you keep calling me Winter?"

I peered at her. "You're not her, are you? I mean, you can't be, but..." I didn't know how to tell her I'd dreamed up Winter.

"I'm not called Winter. Who is she?"

Of course, an avatar I made wouldn't materialize out of thin air. "It doesn't matter. You look like someone I know. Well, someone I created."

"Oh! One of your gaming crushes?" Her dark eyes glinted in amusement.

I nodded as we left the top floor and stopped in the corridor. I tugged on her arm. "Wait! Who are you?"

She tilted her head and grinned. "You can't figure it out? You seem so clever."

"We've never met. I'd remember you. You're stunning."

Her grin widened. "You're not so bad yourself. Way better than your pictures. And after last night, I couldn't stop thinking about you."

"Wait! You're Witch Turner?" This was impossible. Witch Turner looked like my perfect woman. I couldn't believe it.

"Ta-dah! The one and only. Have you got time to talk? I know how crazy busy you are, but I was close by."

"Close by? How did you know where I worked?"

She giggled again. "I have so much to tell you."

"Let's head down a floor. There's an empty breakout room we can use." I couldn't stop staring at her. Witch Turner looked like Winter. How freaky was that? And I still couldn't figure out how she'd found me. Surely, her hacking skills weren't that good. She wouldn't be able to break through Stardust's systems.

Witch Turner kept glancing at me and held my hand as we dashed down the stairs. She was about my age, striking looking, with sharp cheekbones and intelligent eyes. She was dressed in black, just like I imagined Winter always dressed.

"If anyone else was staring at me like that, I'd find it creepy," Witch Turner said.

"Sorry. It's been a crazy day. And you being here has made it even crazier. In here." I accessed the empty breakout room. It was painted sage green and had bean bags and comfy chairs laid out.

I pulled two chairs together and sat in one.

Witch Turner joined me and simply stared into my eyes for several long seconds. "I guess you've got questions."

"So many. How did you find me?"

She gave a little shrug and looked embarrassed. "After we played together last night, I had to know more about you. I felt a connection I'd never had with anyone. Sure, I've gamed with great people, but you seemed different. And we have so much in common. I couldn't sleep, so I used my... skills to find out who you were. I searched the Internet, asked in forums, and someone hinted you were involved in Stardust Industries. After a few hours of hacking, I worked it out. I found your gaming name linked to your real name."

"You hacked Stardust?"

"It's sort of what I do. I hack into places I shouldn't and have fun. I never cause problems, and I'm not a gaming thief. That's not what I'm about. I never usually touch the gaming industry. I'm more into messing with financial institutions and ensuring the fat cats don't get the bonuses they deserve. But I just had to know you." She chewed on her bottom lip. "Does that make me sound weird?"

I gulped and took a moment to take it all in. This was overwhelming, and everything was happening so fast. Haven Witch was coming together. I finally felt happy after a long time of feeling uncertain about my place in the world, and sitting in front of me was my perfect woman.

"Noah, are you going to say anything, or should I walk away with my tail between my legs?"

"What's your real name?"

She let out a sigh. "I'm Sherry. Sherry Brown. I know, not the coolest name, but blame my parents for that. Winter is fun, though. That could be my nickname, although I guess you have that name saved for your dream woman."

Sherry could have it. She was my dream woman. "I like Sherry. It's cute. You're cute. And your hacking skills are insane."

"Thanks, but Sherry is something you drink at Christmas, and only if you're desperate after the decent alcohol has gone." She tilted her head. "You look different from the pictures on the company website. I wasn't sure about using your name earlier in case I'd made a mistake. Your profile picture shows you in a suit and tie with short hair."

I scrubbed my fingers through my beard. "Things are relaxed around here. When I joined, Sylvester insisted we all had a polished corporate image in our pictures. The boss, Gideon, isn't so exacting."

"Sylvester? Is he the sneak?"

"That's the one."

"Why am I not surprised that jerk put you in a suit?" She pinched the sleeve of my sweater. "This is much more your style."

"It was typical Sylvester," I said. "But how did you get inside? Security is tight downstairs, and we had a recent break-in, so everyone's on high alert. At least, I think we did."

Her expression grew coy. "I can't tell you all my secrets, but I may have created an appointment in your calendar and ensured I was on the approved list, so no questions were asked."

"Whoa! You're really good. I'm even more intimidated by you."

She chuckled and caught hold of my hand again, running her thumb over my knuckles several times. "Don't be. I'm all show. I'm more comfortable hiding in my apartment and playing games into the small hours than dealing with all this. I stood outside for half an hour convincing myself I was brave enough to see you."

"I'm so glad you were."

"So am I. That woman I found you with wouldn't have stopped groping you. She was like a hyperactive kraken on speed."

I grimaced. "That was partially my fault. I got this intense smell of honey and followed it to Janis's office. She caught me snooping and got the wrong end of the stick. And I was crouched under her desk when she came in, so I can see how weird it looked. I'm lucky she didn't call the cops on me for lurking."

"She's lucky! You were too much of a gentleman to tell her you didn't want her to jump your bones." Sherry was grinning as she spoke, but it quickly faded. "You didn't want her to jump you, did you? I haven't made a massive mistake by coming here and thinking you were available, have I?"

"No! I was doing my best to let Janis down gently. But how did you know you'd find me in her office?"

"I asked around. Then I saw the door closed and the blinds down and took a look."

"You saved me from a heap of embarrassment," I said. "Thanks."

"Anytime. We protect each other in the games and in real life. Of course, only if you want to." Sherry looked at our joined hands. "I get how weird it is that I just showed up. I hope I'm not a disappointment."

"You're the opposite of a disappointment. You're my dream woman." I blurted the words out before my brain warned me I'd sound like a loser.

Sherry gripped my hand and nodded. "You're amazing, too. And when I figured out who you really were, I was shocked. I knew you were good, but you're at the top of the gaming industry. And your understanding of magic systems and how magic works, it's all I could dream of. All I want to do is hang out with you and play games forever."

My eyebrows shot up. "That's quite a declaration."

"Sorry, I'm being weird and intense again, but I've never felt like this before."

I was about to say me too, when there was a yell, and footsteps dashed past the door. I hurried to the door and opened it. Tegan was running along the corridor, her eyes wide.

"Hey, what's going on?" I said.

She glanced over her shoulder. "Haven't you heard? Sylvester's dead."

# Chapter 11

"How can he be dead? I only saw him this morning." I stepped into the corridor, keeping the door propped open.

"It was a car crash. Gideon sent him out to pick up his lunch order. Sylvester ran a red light, and another car smashed into him. His vehicle was totaled. There was nothing they could do to save him," Tegan said. "Everyone's talking about it."

I glanced over my shoulder at Sherry, who was listening with an impassive look on her face. "I can imagine. Thanks, Tegan."

"I didn't like the guy, but no one would wish him dead. I've got to go. Gideon's in a tailspin. Sylvester's been his right-hand guy for so long, I'm not sure what he'll do without him."

"Yeah, of course." I eased the door shut and turned to face Sherry. "I feel terrible. Just last night, we were planning to destroy Sylvester in a game. Did the universe listen in and make it happen?"

She strode over and caught hold of my hands. "It wasn't the universe who killed him. Let's get out of here while everyone's distracted. There's so much I need to tell you."

"What about Sylvester? Everyone will be in shock. I can't leave."

"No one will notice you're gone. They'll all be gossiping about the crash." She opened the door.

"Don't you feel the tiniest bit bad? I said terrible things about him to you."

"You want me to feel bad for a guy who made your life miserable since you started working here? Not going to happen. Karma comes around to bite everyone in the butt if they deserve it. It was his time. And he did deserve it."

"Sherry, I can't agree with that."

She stood on her tiptoes and kissed me full on the lips. "Let's go. Sylvester's dead, and there's nothing you can do for him by staying here and gossiping with everyone. Focus on us."

I still hesitated, her surprise kiss lingering on my lips.

Sherry kissed me again, and it was so distracting, I couldn't help but respond.

She gently stroked my arm, sending a tingle across my skin. "Don't you want to spend time with me? I put in all the effort to find you. I figured you'd be pleased."

"I am. I'm just so surprised by the bad news about Sylvester." The tingling sensation lingered, and my thoughts grew fuzzy. I shouldn't care about Sylvester.

"He wasn't a good guy. You are. I'm not saying celebrate his death but don't focus on someone who caused you pain. Why do that?"

"You're right. Let's get out of here." I was being an idiot. Sherry was my future, and I couldn't let anything distract me.

We hurried out of the building, and I was pleased Sherry didn't let go of my hand. I liked her looking out for me. It felt good to have someone on my side.

"We can't be too long. I'll need to check on Gideon and make sure he's doing okay. He was harsh on Sylvester but he relied on him," I said.

"You don't need to worry about any of them from now on."

"Sure I do. They're my work family."

"Think about your future, and the future we could have together. It'll be amazing."

"Our... future?"

She flashed me a smile. "Sure. You told me what you wanted last night. Or were those pipe dreams? You were only sweet talking me to get a reaction and make me like you?"

"My plans will happen, but I'm not walking away from all of this now. I'm in the middle of a new game design, and I can't abandon the company after what happened to Sylvester."

"Then look on the positive side of this situation."

"A tragic accident has a positive?"

"Sylvester can't blackmail you now he's dead. Unless he comes back as a ghoul." Sherry grinned at me. "Do you believe in the walking dead?"

A wave of doubt hit me. Sherry was being insensitive and treating death like a joke. She hadn't known Sylvester but could at least act like she cared someone was dead. "I wasn't happy about his behavior, but I'd rather him alive and still blackmailing me than dead in a car crash."

Sherry brushed her hand up and down my arm, and my doubts faded. "Let other people deal with that problem. I want to know all about you. I feel like I've only just scratched the surface."

I tucked her hand in my crooked elbow as we walked around the green space outside the office. I was worrying about nothing. I wanted to be with Sherry. And I wanted to make her happy. "I'm an open book. I'll tell you anything."

"I have to ask, do you think magic is real? I know we talked about it when we were gaming, but could it be possible? The way you create magic in the games, it seems like you know something the rest of us don't."

"I'm not discounting magic. And I've seen enough weird things to think anything is possible."

"Such as?"

"I don't want to tell you. You'll think I'm crazy. You'll run away, and I'll never see you again."

"Don't worry. I've seen plenty of strange things, too. Go on. I'm interested. I always wish our world was more like the worlds in the games we play. It would be much more fun to click your fingers and obliterate the enemy or make them die in a car crash."

I sucked in a breath. "Sherry, that's too soon. Sylvester always drove too fast, but running a red light was reckless. And out of character. He always made out he was so great behind the wheel."

"It must have been the stress of the job. I imagine Gideon is a hard taskmaster. Maybe he pushed Sylvester too hard, so he ended it."

"He had too much of an ego to go out that way. And Sylvester was always showing off about doing an advanced driving course. He claimed he could outrun the police in a high speed pursuit."

"Braggy douche. Actions speak louder than words. Sylvester could brag all he liked, but he's the one dead because he didn't see a red light."

I looked at the office. "I should get back and see if Gideon needs anything."

"Wait! One more minute. You can't leave me hanging. You told me you thought magic was possible but won't reveal why, other than saying you've seen strange things. Is that it?" Sherry did that calming stroke down my arm again, making me forget about the office.

I walked with her in silence for a minute, trying to figure out how to let Sherry know about my visions and hallucinations without making her run off. "I need to come clean with you. I really like you, but I've got issues. I've been seeing therapists to figure things out for a while, but nothing works."

She didn't react with horror or shock. "Do you want to tell me why you're in therapy?"

I didn't want her thinking I was a weirdo, but Sherry deserved the truth.

She leaned against my arm. "I won't judge. But I always appreciate full disclosure."

I ran a hand down my face. "It started with a sense I was being watched. That was maybe a year ago. I ignored it at first. Gideon always talks about watching our backs and making sure no one steals the concepts or takes advantage of us."

"Of course he does. The gaming industry is worth billions."

"I figured I'd gotten freaked out by what he told us. He mentions it in every weekly briefing, so I started thinking people were watching me."

"Anything else?"

"I've been having intense dreams about the characters in the games. Well, one character in particular. This'll sound dumb, but I've lost my heart to a fictional witch. Winter. And when you showed up at the office, I was convinced you were her. You look just like I imagined her to be."

"I look like the woman of your dreams?" Sherry grinned up at me.

I chuckled. "You do. You shocked the heck out of me." We kept walking, and I kept putting the weird experiences I'd had together in the least freaky way possible. "I've also been experiencing strange symptoms. I've thought a couple of times that I've floated, or I've made things float."

"Wow! That does sound like magic."

"Don't tease."

"I'm not. People believe, see, and experience curious things. Things that can't be explained away." She tugged on my arm. "I believe there's more to this world than meets the eye. If you believe you made something float, then maybe you did. Did anything happen just before the things floated?"

"The first time, a weird spark shot out of my hand."

Her eyes widened. "Interesting. I wonder why?"

"No idea. But when I tried to do it again, nothing happened. The weirdest thing was when I fell asleep at my desk. When I woke, I was floating above it."

"This gets better. You are brimming with magic."

"You promise you're not teasing?"

"No! I'm interested. And I'm listening."

"Good, because I'm not sure I could share something like that with my therapist."

"You don't need therapy. There's nothing wrong with you."

"It feels like there is. Because there's more. I think... I breathed fire. I set fire to my office building."

Sherry clapped her hands together. "You're extraordinary. You're more than I could ever have hoped for."

"You want a guy who thinks he can breathe fire and floats?"

"You can do a lot more than that. And you're just getting started."

"I don't want any of this. I don't even want the feelings of paranoia, but I'll take them if that's the only symptom. Add in the red glitter that keeps appearing and the weird enhanced sense of smell I've developed recently, and I'm a lost cause."

"You're not lost. You're finding yourself. I'm sure there'll be road bumps, but you can handle them. And I'll be with you, so I'll make sure you're properly looked after."

"That's nice of you, but I need to handle this on my own. And I don't want us to get involved if I've got issues to work through. Maybe it's a brain thing.

A growth or something. It could be causing all of this."

"It's not a growth. You're not sick. And I think you're amazing. Fire Fang, I've been looking for you for such a long time."

I chuckled. "You can call me Noah outside of the game."

"I love Fire Fang, though. It suits you."

I shrugged. "Sure. You really think I'm okay, even after everything I told you?"

"More than okay. You're perfect." Sherry gripped my arm and slid her fingers down to circle my wrist.

"I think you're perfect, too. And it's just like magic that you showed up in my life when I needed you the most. Did you cast a spell over me?" The ache in my chest making me want to kiss her again suggested I'd been struck with a love potion.

"You think I'm magical?" She fluttered her lashes at me.

"It explains why you're here, being calm about all the weird things I'm telling you. And you're so beautiful. You're my dream woman."

Sherry giggled. "You'll be asking me to move in with you next."

I hesitated and looked at her. I'd spent my life hiding behind games and never living a full life. I wanted it all. I wanted my dream business in the country, the wife, the children, and the animals running around. And I was done holding back and doubting myself. I needed to take a leap and make a change.

"You okay? What's going on behind those lovely eyes?" Sherry said.

I turned to face her, got down on one knee, and caught hold of her hand. "This will prove I'm a total weirdo, but hear me out before breaking my heart."

Her eyes widened, and she nodded. "I'm listening."

"You're amazing. Why shouldn't we move in together? I've got a great apartment you can share with me, and we've got so much in common. How could it go wrong?"

Her mouth fell open. "Well, we both love games and believe in magic. Is that enough?"

"It's more than that. You're kind, smart, and funny, and you didn't flinch when I told you about floating above my desk and having paranoia. I know this will work. I can't imagine not having you in my life. Not now I found you—"

"I actually found you, thanks to my hacking skills."

I grinned up at her. "Thanks to your excellent hacking skills, this has become real. We have the chance of an amazing future together. What do you think? Move in with me. Let's make magic together."

"Fire Fang, you're adorable. My sisters had their doubts, but I knew you'd be the perfect subject."

"Subject?"

She tugged me to my feet and kissed me again, her lip balm leaving behind a hint of sweet honey. "You're just what I've been looking for."

"You've been talking about me to your sisters?"

"Yes. They want to know everything about you. They didn't think you'd be strong enough, but I had a sense you'd fit right in. I sensed the wild animal beneath the calm front you present to the world."

"Wild animal?" I tried to let go of her hand, but she held on. "I don't understand."

She stroked her free hand slowly up and down my arm again, soothing my doubt. "Some things, you just know. Now, we must seal our arrangement. I've brought something for you to try. The final piece in the puzzle."

"What about my question? Would you like to move in? Is that what you mean?"

Her nose wrinkled. "Something like that. You can move in with me, though. I've got the perfect place for you. It's out of the way, so we won't be bothered. Lots of space and places to hide and conduct our magic."

For a second, her face shimmered, and I got a glimpse of something dark that made my spine tense. "I'd need to check your place to make sure I can work from there."

"You won't care about work soon." Sherry held out her hand. There was a piece of pale pink candy on her palm. "I made this for you."

"You did? Just for me?" I focused on her face, but whatever I'd seen had gone. Another unwanted hallucination hitting at the worst moment.

She nodded. "Handcrafted, so you know it's full of love and a dash of magic."

"Magic, huh?" I wasn't in the mood for anything sweet, but I didn't want to disappoint Sherry. I lifted the candy and took a bite.

She gasped and clasped her hands together. "How do you feel?"

"It's good. Really sweet." The candy was soft, with tiny nutty pieces in it.

Her forehead wrinkled. "Anything else?"

"I'm not good with flavors. Maybe honey? Although that could be your lip balm."

"Finish it. I have to know you enjoy it."

I put the last of the candy in my mouth and chewed. A tingle of heat spiraled down my throat and into my chest. It made me feel cold and then hot. "That was different. What have you got in here, popping candy?"

"You're feeling it, aren't you? I knew I got the balance right. Of course, the work I've been doing to lead up to this moment has helped." She let go of my hand and twirled. There was a flash of pink and yellow, and the honey smell strengthened.

"Work for what?" I rubbed my stomach. Sugar didn't agree with me.

"For your new future. Our future. I've tried so many times to get this right. This plan was always more than making my candy magic perfect. It was about finding you. Finding someone who was open to believing. And after watching you and following you for so long, I knew you'd survive my tests."

"You've been following me?" I took a step back. "And what am I meant to survive?"

"One more candy! That should do the trick. All your worries will fade." Sherry held out her hand to reveal a second pink candy. Where had that come from?

I reached for it, even though I didn't want it. My stomach churned, and waves of freezing cold alternating with burning heat fired through me. I held the candy in front of me, my hand shaking.

My brain was telling me not to eat this. Something terrible would happen if I did.

"Let me help." Sherry grabbed the candy and shoved it between my lips.

For a second, she looked different. Her hair was long and matted. Her eyes were black, and her fingers looked too long to be human. She also wore the same frilly dress the intruder had worn. I blinked, and Sherry had returned to normal.

It was my eyes. Or my head. I couldn't lose control now. Not when I was so close to getting everything I wanted.

"What are you waiting for? You'll upset me if you don't eat my candy. Take a bite."

I took the candy in my mouth, chewed, and swallowed. More weird energy flooded through me, and I staggered back, my vision blurring as pain flooded my joints. I didn't want to stand and buckled over in agony.

When my gaze refocused and I looked up, Sherry was gone. A strange, pale creature with purple veins throbbing under her skin and black spirals swirling around her floated before me. Her feet were several inches off the ground, and silky black coverings shrouded her thin form.

"How do you feel, my little pup?" the creature whispered. "Ready to bark for me?"

"Where's Sherry?" The words came out rough and croaky.

"I'm right here, sweetie pup. This is your Sherry. Want another kiss?"

I howled an unearthly sound as my bones broke and my memories blurred. This felt too painful to be another hallucination. Was I dying? Was there something wrong with the candy? Had Sherry poisoned me?

The monstrous version of Sherry placed an icy hand on my forehead. "Shush, don't be afraid, Fire Fang. Your magical dreams are about to come true. You should be happy."

I snarled out my pain, unable to speak.

She leaned in close. "Let me tell you a secret. Magic is very real, very dark, and very dangerous. I do hope you'll survive my little spell. I've worked so hard to find an obedient mortal who'd die for me and my candy."

As I fell to my hands and knees, my bones splintering and reforming, fur sprouting all over my body, and my teeth elongating, I knew her words were true. Magic was real, and not all of it was good.

Whatever power had me was about to change me forever. Would I survive this?

As the blackness took me and Sherry's cruel laugh shook around me, I held on to one word. A single word that left a seed of hope in my throbbing heart: Winter.

# What's next?

I couldn't resist writing one more mystery for you. Silvaria Digby's origin story has been keeping me awake. What made her so jaded? Just how powerful is she? And where does her love of dance come from?

Get ready. Silvaria explains it all.

**A future that cannot be escaped, a tragic death, and a race to uncover the truth.**

I love pretty dresses, planning my upcoming marriage to my delectable fiancé, and figuring out how I'll become a famous dancer.

Corpses don't feature in those plans.

Unfortunately, my parents, the corpses, and my grave magic have other ideas!

I've inherited a power I never wanted, but it wants me. And when my friend, and servant, is murdered in my home and her corpse returns with a plea for justice, I cannot ignore my power. How will I balance my dreams with my family's harsh expectations of me becoming a cemetery guardian, my fiancé's desire for me to abandon the corpses forever, and the demands of the Magic Council who are investigating (poorly) my dear friend's murder?

This is Silvaria Digby's origin story. Set in a quaintly historical past in a world not far from the Witch Haven you know and love, where balls, bonnets, and carriages are all the rage. Enjoy spending time with our powerful future cemetery guardian as she tackles difficult home life, shambling bodies, and a murder that's too close to home.

Get your copy of **Silvaria** today!

Want a free peek? Keep turning the pages.

# About Author

K.E. O'Connor (Karen) is a mystery author living in the beautiful British countryside. She loves all things mystery, animals, and cake.

If you want to be part of the Witch Haven crew, practice spells, solve a few murders, spend time with amazing witches and their talking familiars, and get a free book, join her weekly newsletter.

Sign up today.

**Newsletter:**
https://BookHip.com/QKGDWJW
**Website:**
www.keoconnor.com/writing
**Facebook:**
www.facebook.com/keoconnorauthor

# Also By

**Witch Haven:** Welcome to Witch Haven, where nothing is what it seems. Meet four fabulous witches as they struggle with their destinies, deal with misfiring magic, murder, and the irksome Magic Council.

**Crypt Witches:** Meet Tempest Crypt, a witch who swallows demons, and Wiggles, her talking hellhound, while you enjoy magical murder and intrigue.

**Lorna Shadow:** A cozy mystery series set in the fun world of a personal assistant who sees ghosts. Meet Lorna, her ditzy sidekick, Helen, and Flipper, the dog who senses ghosts, as they solve crimes and save the day.

**Holly Holmes:** An adorable cozy culinary mystery series set in the beautiful English village of Audley St. Mary. Each book is full of treats, murder, and twists. Join Holly and Meatball, her clue-hunting dog, as they solve murders and eat cake.

If you enjoyed

*Fire Fang*

turn the page to read an extract from the next
Witch Haven mystery. This is Silvaria Digby's origin
story. Set in a quaintly historical past in a world
not far from the Witch Haven you know and love,
where balls, bonnets, and carriages are all the
rage. Enjoy spending time with our powerful future
cemetery guardian as she tackles difficult home life,
shambling bodies, and a murder that's too close to
home.

## SILVARIA

# Chapter 1

"I hope we won't talk about dead bodies all night." My tall, broad-shouldered, classically handsome fiancé, Emory Farr, adjusted his high-starched collar, inching a finger in between the fabric and his neck.

"Aunt Ruby will expect some discussion about corpses. It's only polite." I smoothed the pale pink silk of my new corseted dress over my knees. It had a charming sweetheart neckline, long lace sleeves, and the hem brushed the floor as I walked. Aunt Ruby was old-fashioned in every sense. Too much flesh on display, and she wouldn't talk to you.

"Not all of us find the dead as fascinating as your family." Emory stopped tugging at his collar and settled into the plush red velvet cushions in the carriage as it trundled toward my aunt's estate on the edge of Briar Pass.

"Marry me, marry into the Digby's world of the undead." I tried to make light of my family's long history as cemetery guardians, but it wasn't for everyone. Including me. Many found our work morbid, and controlling corpses wasn't an ability I'd ever wanted. But some things in life couldn't be chosen. They just were.

Emory's sigh sounded like he was in pain. "Silvaria, darling, I do understand. And I'll fake an interest and talk to the old girl about dead things, but change the subject as soon as you think it's polite."

"Of course." I reached over and adjusted his pink silk cravat. It matched my dress.

He gently pulled my hand away but kept hold of it. "Stop fussing. I've handled worse dragons than your aunt Ruby."

"She can be difficult, and this is the first time you've visited her estate. Aunt Ruby is old and set in her ways. And we mustn't be late. Dinner is on the table at six sharp."

"We won't be late. I don't know why you're so intent on impressing her. It's not as if you need her money."

"Emory! That's not why we're visiting. She's my only living aunt. I like to check in on her and make sure she's well. She's become isolated as she's gotten older and spends more time with the corpses than anyone else."

"Isn't that your family's motto? You prefer the dead to the living. Vivos praeferre mortuos?"

I swatted his arm. "Don't tease. And it's not that. It's Memento mori. Remember, we all die, so we treat the corpses with respect because we'll become one eventually."

He placed an arm around my shoulders, sending a small thrill down my spine. "I'll be on my best behavior. Even your frosty old aunt will be enchanted by me by the end of the evening."

"She said she won't come to our wedding." I leaned into his embrace. I felt so lucky to have such a handsome, clever man to marry. It wasn't easy to find someone who accepted my unusual, and unwanted, ability to control the dead. Many people found my family's talent as cemetery guardians creepy. Some actively avoided them. But we were an essential part of the magical community. If the dead weren't cared for, they rose and rioted.

Emory had seen past all of that. Of course, he'd been wary when we started dating, but he was comfortable with my heritage. Me, not so much.

"If your aunt doesn't want to come to the wedding, she can stay in her manor house and dance with the corpses if she likes. Nothing will spoil our big day," Emory said.

"I would love her to be there, though. Perhaps that's what she needs, a break from the morbid life she's built. Well, it's more like a morbid half-life. She talks about the bodies more than she does her family."

"If your aunt Ruby causes problems for us, we'll distance ourselves from her. We'll both be ridiculously wealthy soon enough, so we can do whatever we want. You already have your trust fund, and my business plans are on the up, so it's not as if we need to fake charm the old lady out of her fortune."

I sat up straight and glared at him. "I hope that was a joke. Aunt Ruby may be rich, but that's not the reason I keep in touch."

He arched a thick eyebrow. "Then you're better than most. What do you get out of this relationship? She browbeats you every time you visit, and her default position is to complain."

I clasped my gloved hands in my lap. "Aunt Ruby was different when she was younger. I even remember her playing with me when I was a child. I can't imagine her doing that now. It's the power, you see. It drains you."

Emory chuckled. "She'd probably feed you to one of her pet corpses if you were still small."

"She does not have pet corpses in the house." He got another smack on the arm for that comment.

"Darling, I'm teasing. All I meant was, even if your aunt doesn't approve of what we're doing, we'll still be blissfully happy. We have the world at our feet. We could move to another country, build our own enormous manor house in the countryside, or buy a home somewhere warmer."

"And fill those homes with children?" I'd always wanted a big family, and Emory was the same. We'd talked for hours about how we'd create a household full of laughter and brimming with life. It was something I'd never experienced when growing up.

"Of course. Whatever your heart desires."

I sighed and rested against him, smiling at the future within reach. My childhood had been surrounded by groaning corpses and the restless dead. It wasn't something I'd recommend to anybody.

All I'd wanted when I was younger was to be loved and included, but my parents were as obsessed with corpses as Aunt Ruby. They definitely lived by the family motto of preferring the dead to the living and were quick to remind me of my own mortality.

When we started our family, I'd make sure none of my children ever felt unloved or uncertain about their place in the household.

"We're almost there." Emory looked out the window as the carriage turned and the horses passed between two large, open black gates.

"Aunt Ruby will grow to adore you almost as much as I do. Just give her a few hours to thaw. She won't be able to resist you for long, especially since you look so handsome in your new suit."

"It is an excellent cut. You spoil me, darling. I didn't need another suit. You bought me two last month."

"You said you liked the tailoring when we stopped to look in the Saville's storefront. And you had to look your best. Aunt Ruby would expect nothing less. Besides, I enjoy treating you." I smoothed his cravat again.

He pressed a soft kiss against one of my powdered cheeks. "You're a sweetheart. I'm so happy we have each other."

So was I, and I still had to pinch myself to be certain this was real. Emory could have had his pick of the ladies, but he'd chosen me. When we'd met at the Countess of Eden's winter ball six months ago, everything had fallen into place. He'd only danced with two other ladies that evening and spent the rest of it with me. I'd left the ball giddy and hopelessly in love. Our relationship had only gotten better from there, and our future together would be amazing.

The carriage pulled up after a slow meander along my aunt's gravel driveway. Despite living alone, she maintained one of the three family manor houses as her private residence. The house was a pale sandstone detached building with a dark roof, elaborate chimney stacks, and twelve bedrooms.

I'd suggested she downsize, but she'd dismissed my comment. Family values had to be maintained, and everyone knew the estate belonged to the Digbys. That would never change.

I'd learned to keep quiet with my aunt and my parents over matters of propriety. They were sticklers for formality and reputation. Nothing was more important. Not even the happiness of their only daughter.

Emory climbed out of the carriage and held out his hand to allow me to disembark. My silk dress was stunning but difficult to move in. There was a large bustle on the back, and the fitted long shift under the dress meant I could only take tiny steps to avoid toppling, so I was grateful for Emory's arm as we headed to the black front door with its brass knocker.

The door opened on its own, and we stepped inside. The entrance hall had a cold marble floor, and several urns containing former cemetery guardian ashes stood on either side of the door.

Emory's gaze was full of interest as he looked around the high-ceilinged hallway. "It must cost a fortune to keep this place warm."

"It does, but my aunt prefers it chilly." I coughed delicately into my hand. "She often has undead visitors, and they decay slower if it's cold. It's why

I told you to wear a thermal layer underneath your suit."

"Does she often have corpses visit?" Horror flickered in his eyes for a second.

"More often than she should." Approaching footsteps had me looking up, and Aunt Ruby strode toward us.

Despite her advanced years, having survived three hundred and fifty of them, she had a firm, steady pace, and her back was straight. Her skin was paled and lined and her purple eyes watery, but the power radiating off her tingled against my skin.

She stepped forward to greet me first with two light air kisses on either cheek, making sure not to smudge my makeup or disrupt my elaborate dark curls. "You have stayed away too long, niece. I barely recognize you." Her gaze ran over me several times. "You look thin."

"I want to look my best at the wedding."

She glared at me as if I'd said something stupid and then did a thorough visual inspection of Emory. "He's too handsome for a plain Jane like you. I never trust a face so perfectly symmetrical."

Emory softly cleared his throat. "It's a great honor to meet you again. I've heard so much about your incredible work from Silvaria. She treasures your talent with the... dead."

My aunt harrumphed. "I doubt that very much. My niece has yet to take to her role as a cemetery guardian, but time will mature her, and she'll see this is the only path. This way. Dinner is about to be served."

I raised my eyebrows at Emory, my cheeks hot with embarrassment at being talked about as if I wasn't present, but his smile was calm, and it reassured me as we headed into the dining room.

The room was an austere work of art, with a mosaic floor that had been removed piece by piece from a Roman amphitheater and reconstructed inside the manor house. Original tapestries from the reign of Queen Hilda covered most of the walls, depicting countryside scenes and the occasional bloody battle. A large black dining table dominated the center of the room. There were twenty chairs around it, but my aunt always sat at the head of the table and her guests in the seats closest to her.

She stood by her seat and waited for her butler to pull out the chair. Once we were settled, three servers came in with plates covered in silver domes.

They presented my aunt with her food. She glared at it as if it had done something wrong to her then cut off a small piece of chicken and tasted it. "It's dry. Tell Cook to be more careful."

"Shall I take it back?" The serving girl's hand shook slightly.

"It's fine. Leave us." My aunt glared at the servers until they'd left the room. "Emory, pour the wine."

He hopped from his seat and filled our glasses.

My aunt took a sip and winced. "Sharp. I need to clear the wine cellar and start again. I'm sure it's not being stored appropriately. The servants don't know what they're doing."

I took a small sip from my glass. "It's good, and dinner looks lovely."

My aunt ignored my comments, took several small bites, and then pushed her plate away. "I have no appetite for bland fare. I should get someone who knows what they're doing in my kitchen."

"It's excellent food," Emory said.

My aunt turned an acerbic look on him. "Silvaria tells me you're in trade."

"No! Not trade. Emory is an entrepreneur. He has many business ideas. Wonderful ideas," I said.

"Ideas? Do you have any form of employment?" My aunt peered down her long, thin nose at him.

Emory carefully set down his knife and fork as a gentle pink flush spread up his neck and onto his cheeks. "I've tried several businesses over the years but have recently settled on property development. There will always be a need for people to have safe, warm places to live. Just today, my new business partner and I visited a potential site for future development."

"I didn't know about that. How exciting," I said.

Aunt Ruby didn't look impressed. "That's an occupation of sorts. Of course, when you marry Silvaria, you will assist her. My first husband was my assistant. He gathered the grave dirt, met with the families who were having troubles, and dealt with the paperwork."

"Oh, no. That won't work!"

Aunt Ruby silenced me with a sharp look. "And my last husband, Yanez, had an affinity with the dead. That was useful. Do you have any natural ability with our clients, Mr. Farr?"

Emory shuffled in his seat. "My magic is more a secondary concern of mine."

Alarm flickered in my aunt's eyes. "You have power, though?"

"He does. Emory is incredible with people and makes everyone feel comfortable in all situations. It's a real talent," I said.

Aunt Ruby pushed her food around the plate with her fork. "Silvaria's always been socially awkward. Having a natural charmer by her side should smooth over her stiffness."

My cheeks flushed again, and I busied myself with cutting into some tender stem broccoli. I struggled in the company of others but tried hard to fit in. People gossiped about my ability with the dead, and I'd even had a few individuals ask if I could provide them with a corpse for entertainment. What a dreadful thought.

"Have your parents chosen you a cemetery yet?" Aunt Ruby said. "I have several suggestions if they're struggling to settle on one."

I almost choked on my broccoli and took several sips of wine to help regain my composure. "Not yet. They're still considering my options."

"They've kept you coddled. You must take up the mantel of guardian. I was eighteen when I took on my first cemetery. If you don't have a placement soon, you'll forget how to look after the dead."

"We were planning on finding a situation close to my first development project," Emory said. "That way, Silvaria can tend to her cemetery guardian duties while I work."

"Putting your future husband's needs before the dead is unwise," Aunt Ruby said. "I married five times and picked my partners because of their affinity with the dead. You should marry a half-vampire, Silvaria. They like the quiet of the night and would enjoy their time in the cemeteries you tend to."

I gulped down my panic. I hadn't yet had the courage to tell my family I didn't want to be a cemetery guardian. The dead left me cold in every sense. I hated everything about being born into a guardian family. I hated the headstones, the eerie silence as I walked among the crypts and sarcophagi, the stench of rot and decay, the dirt, and the ever present feeling of something stirring beneath my feet, waiting for a command.

Being a cemetery guardian was a dismal life, and having parents who were guardians had ruined my childhood. I was only awkward because we kept to ourselves, and when another child found out what I could do, they ran away and didn't want to be friends with a corpse tender.

Aunt Ruby clicked her fingers. "I've always loved the power and control. When a corpse misbehaves, I'm there to take them in hand. Show me what you've got."

"I'm sorry?" I said.

She clicked her fingers again, and the door leading out to the herb garden opened.

Emory lurched from his seat with a yelp as a bedraggled corpse missing an arm appeared.

"Calm yourself, boy. You'll have to get used to this if you're marrying into the family."

"Aunt! No corpses in the dining room. We're eating." I jumped up too, alarmed at Emory's panic.

He'd seen plenty of corpses when he was with me, so he shouldn't be so startled.

"If you want the corpse gone, you deal with him," Aunt Ruby said, a sly smile on her face.

Emory backed away. "Silvaria, do something. It's looking at me strangely."

I pleaded silently with my aunt, staring at her and clasping my hands, but she wouldn't acknowledge me. She sipped her wine and gave me another cold smile.

I held out my hands, grimacing as the cold flood of power ran through me. "Return to where you came from. Your presence is not wanted."

The corpse groaned, turned, and ambled back into the herb garden.

I rushed over and slammed the door shut. I whirled toward my aunt. "What are you doing with bodies in your backyard? He had fresh dirt on him. Does he sleep here?"

She gave a small shrug. "It's always good to keep your hand in, and I like to have subjects close by. The walking dead are a valuable asset."

I shook my head at her. My family was unbelievable. No wonder everyone gossiped about us.

"Don't look so scandalized." Aunt Ruby gestured at my chair. "This is your destiny. Marry a tradesman if you must, but your cemetery guardian duties will always come first."

I returned to my seat after checking Emory wasn't about to collapse in shock.

Aunt Ruby was wrong. I made my own destiny. And it didn't involve dead bodies at the dining table.